TINSEL AND TEACUPS

HOLIDAY BEACH SWEET ROMANCE
BOOK 3

ELLE RUSH

Cover by Elizabeth Mackey

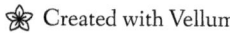 Created with Vellum

To Ross, my favourite Christmas elf

BOOKS INCLUDED IN TINSEL AND TEACUPS

Tinsel and Teacups
Sweet Christmas
The Christmas Tree Caper
Ring in the New Year

PART ONE

TINSEL AND TEACUPS

Barista Rachel Best has a lot on her tea saucer. Besides all the usual Christmas activities, she's falling behind on organizing her food bank fundraiser. Her biggest problem is a handsome antiques dealer who keeps interfering with her raffle prizes.

Owen Daye has been too busy taking over the family business and being a father to his young son to realize that he's made an enemy of the cute coffee shop owner, but when his grandfather volunteers him to work with Rachel, sparks fly.

Can they put aside their battle to find the perfect teacup long enough make sure that the charity auction goes off without a hitch, or will the Christmas spirit of Holiday Beach fail when it's needed most?

CHAPTER 1

THAT NO-GOOD, treasure-stealing antique hunter was already here.

She could smell it.

What Rachel Best actually smelled was the combination of a woodsy aftershave and leather with a hint of dust, but she knew what that meant. Owen Daye was already at the Christmas craft and antique sale, swooping in and snatching up the best finds of the day.

She'd travelled far and wide over the last few months, but as usual, the biggest sale of them all was at the River Street Community Center in her hometown of Holiday Beach. People flocked from all over northern Minnesota for the best Christmas present buying opportunities in the county. They filled the parking lot, laughing as they tromped through ankle-high drifts. In another month, they'd be grumbling about having to shovel the same snow, but right now, winter was fresh on the scene, and the Christmas decorations on every building sparked holiday cheer in everyone who saw them.

Rachel would appreciate the scenery on another day.

Her flat tire meant that her archrival had thirty extra minutes to scout the deals. But she wouldn't let that setback defeat her. She was a woman on a mission.

The last antique sale of the season was always hit or miss. Some people slapped an antique label on all the old junk they'd found over the spring and summer as they'd cleaned out garages and cottages. It was the others she came for, the ones who catered to real antique buyers. Rachel might get lucky at a table from the first group, but like Owen, she needed an authentic dealer.

She had to go by instinct when she shopped, but Owen was a professional, which gave him a slight edge. She'd begrudgingly admit that he knew his stuff. He'd begun managing his grandfather's business in Holiday Beach over the summer, and was at the community center to buy furniture, vintage clothes, and knickknacks for Golden Daye Antiques. He was welcome to it all, with one exception.

Teacups.

Yes, she owned a coffee shop. The best coffee shop in Holiday Beach, in her mostly unbiased opinion. By the Cup served caffeinated creations in custom-made maroon mugs with granite gray interiors so she had no need for the teacups for her business. She was on a hunt for fine bone china for totally altruistic reasons, and to make sure she got the best of the best the sale had to offer, she needed to beat Owen to the punch.

Rachel quickly glanced around the hall and saw several tables filled with possibilities on either side of the room. She let herself get caught in the flow of bargain seekers and drifted down the first row. A stand filled with colorful Pyrex cookware caught her eye, but she forced herself to move past it without slowing. She hesitated beside a collection of glass cases filled with vintage paste jewelry that was calling her name, but she steeled her resolve and kept going.

There! On the last table before the double-wide home-made fudge and nuts booth on the corner. She saw some Old Country Roses fruit cups on a shelf, and a Spode Blue Italian platter on display. There was bound to be an odd teacup and saucer in the mix. Most people needed to pick up a replacement piece to a certain pattern to complete a set, but Rachel wanted the odd, unmatched ones because they were notable. Memorable.

She saw a Lenox Holiday teacup at the far end of the table. *Perfect.* The creamy cup with delicate sprigs of mistletoe cried out for her to buy it. She skirted the woman with double stroller, went wide around the man carrying a six-foot-tall wooden giraffe, and ducked back into the table. And somehow, in those three seconds, her prize had vanished. She saw it floating above the table, attached to a hand attached to an arm in the sleeve of a leather jacket she recognized. "Owen," she growled.

"Good morning, Rachel." He sounded friendly, but the twinkle in his green eyes had a sparkle that was mocking her. He had to look down at her because he was so much taller, which only annoyed her more. "What are you doing here?"

"Not buying that Holiday teacup, apparently."

"You've got to be fast in the antiques game."

"Did you leave any teacups behind for the rest of us?" It was a game they'd been playing at every antique show throughout the summer and fall. Unfortunately, she'd come up the loser more often than not.

"Probably as many as you left for me at the sale in Bixby last month. Vintage china is a rough business. This beauty's a real find, isn't it?" Owen beamed. "We can't keep stuff like this in stock. This particular piece is going to finish a place setting I have back at the store. Do you collect this pattern?"

"Not specifically," she admitted.

"How about the Spode?" he asked, pointing at the platter.

"Not a chance."

He handed the cup and saucer to the vendor, then lifted the huge platter to inspect it more closely. "This place has been a goldmine today." He pointed over his shoulder. "I cleaned out a stall back there. They had a Botanical Gardens sugar and creamer pair. I also got three of their lead crystal snifter sets, and two Rolling Stones albums." He turned the platter over and checked the stamp on the bottom. "I'll take this too," he said.

"We had quite the selection of vinyl last year, but we decided that china was more profitable and sold it all off in the spring. But I'm glad to see that Golden Daye Antiques is keeping a broad variety of stock for the store. You are Goldie's grandson, aren't you?" The woman didn't wait for an answer. "He's such a dear. I was pleased to hear he's on the mend." Without taking a breath, she continued. "This sale is a great start to my morning. Can I interest you in anything else?" she asked as she reach behind the table reached for a large sheet of bubble wrap.

Rachel watched the vendor hand over a large paper bag with the wrapped cup, saucer and platter in it. When Owen added it to the three other bags he was already holding, an idea began to form. If the vendor was feeling chatty, she could slow down Rachel's competition for a while. "Actually, my good friend is Goldie's grandson, and he's desperately on the lookout for other one-of-a-kind pieces. He'd like to hear about everything you have." She winked at the woman while slapping him on the shoulder. "I'll bet you find all sorts of treasures here, Owen. I'm going to check out the far wall while you shop here and take a trip back to your car to drop off all your goodies. Don't worry, I'll leave one or two teacups for you. Maybe."

She dodged shoppers as she strode through the aisles, wearing a triumphant grin. With Owen tied up, she gave herself a few extra seconds at each table, her eyes peeled for her next find. Unfortunately, her cunning plan didn't work as well as she'd hoped. Soup bowls, candy dishes, and teapots abounded, but the prize she was after was elusive. Didn't the vendors know she had a deadline? "My kingdom for a decent teacup," she muttered to herself when all she found was yet another floral-patterned cup that she'd seen a hundred times already.

Finally, in the middle of the last row, she found something worthy of her attention. A current of air came from behind her. "Forget it, Owen. I'm calling dibs on the butterfly," she said in warning.

His soft chuckle was right in her ear. "Are you sure you want that old thing?"

"Definitely." She squeezed past the tall woman looking at a ceramic cow creamer, then carefully picked up the cup and saucer. Rachel had seen pictures of butterfly teacups before, where a delicate butterfly took the place of a handle. This one was spring pink with a monarch handle, and the saucer was fluted like flower-petals in a matching pink with gold trim. If it was the only thing that she purchased today, it would be worth the trip. She didn't see any chips or cracks, so she carefully set the cup back on the saucer. "How much are you asking?"

The answer made her swallow hard. But it was such a good piece she couldn't walk away. Not when Owen would snap it up the second that she put it down. "I'll take it."

"Great find, Rachel. You'll be happy with that," he said. He had some nerve, being a good sport about losing out on such a treasure.

"Thanks."

The truth was that although she was happy with it, she wouldn't be happy with it for long. That was the whole point. That teacup and eleven other unique ones like it were only going to be in her hands for another month. Then she was going to pass them on to others who wanted them, or just wanted to do a good deed in the spirit of Christmas.

In the four years she'd owned By the Cup, Rachel had been fortunate enough to do a booming business in the summer. Holiday Beach, Minnesota, was a vacation destination that specialized in going all out for the holidays. From Memorial Day to Labor Day, the town was full of campers and tourists. Their Independence Day celebrations lasted for nearly a week.

For the other nine months of the year, she stayed afloat thanks to the town's year-round residents and visitors who came in for the various special events on the calendar. But like in many resort towns, the off-season lasted much too long compared to what people had saved while things were good. In the spirit of community and giving, Rachel had decided to do what she could to help.

Throughout the year, she collected rare, memorable, or outright wacky teacups from antique sales around the state. Then, in December, she displayed them around the coffee shop and let people bid on them in a silent auction.

The winning bid got to take home the cup filled with their beverage of choice. Her Cup of Cheer fundraiser was a small one, but the donation she made to the food bank ensured a few local families got through the long winter better than they otherwise would have.

For the first three years, Goldie Daye had been her partner in crime. Owen's grandfather had set aside a few teacups that he acquired here and there and sold them to her at cost so she could have some exciting options for people to admire and compete for. Sadly, since a bad fall had sent him into semi-retirement in the summer, Rachel hadn't been able to visit him. She'd approached Owen, who had taken over the store, to see if he was interested in partnering with her for the event, but he'd hadn't responded to any of her messages. She'd given him a pass for the first few months, letting him get settled in a new house, town, and job, but after he'd ignored her the last time, she let that idea go and decided to move ahead on her own.

This butterfly teacup was number eleven. She needed one more, and she'd finally be done. But the tables had turned against her again. Owen was empty-handed and able to move easily through the crowd, while she was laden with packages. She'd only purchased the one teacup, but when she'd seen an entire section of hard-boiled detective paperbacks on a table of used books, she'd loaded up and bought two grocery bags full.

Rachel didn't expect to find anything else, not with only a dozen booths left to investigate. One of them held shoebox after shoebox of sports and gaming cards. Another table was full of military memorabilia. The colorful one beside it held stacks of crocheted baby clothes and piles of knit caps.

And then, at the table she would have seen first if she had turned right instead of left when she first walked through the doors, she saw it.

It called to her, shining like a beacon of all that was beautiful and right in the world.

A Prairie Pioneer cup and saucer.

Right there. In Holiday Beach. Like it wasn't an extraordinary event that needed an announcement trumpeted around the entire town and a private spotlight to shine on its glory.

Rachel froze in the middle of the aisle, auction forgotten. She'd seen a picture of a Prairie Pioneer before, a faded photograph that hadn't done it justice now that she'd seen one in person. It wasn't pretty or popular, but it was memorable and unique. It was thicker than a standard teacup. Similar to a pottery mug, it was made of clay. But what made it truly special was its design; it was formed and fired all as one piece, so taking a sip of tea meant the drinker could hold it by the cup or by the saucer.

The style didn't last long. Her own knowledge and further personal research indicated the Prairie Pioneer was only popular for a few years in the 1930s, probably because most folks in the Great Depression were too broke to buy fancy, breakable china. But Rachel had always loved the practical idea behind the unique design.

This particular sample was granite gray cup with a royal blue saucer, both flecked with black and white specks. It had an extra-wide loop in the handle for convenient gripping, unlike some of the tiny bone china ones that were too small to actually use.

There were rumors about an even more exclusive variety of Prairie Pioneer teacups: a set of minis the creator put out each December when the regular cups had been in production. The minis were strictly ornamental, smaller than espresso cups, and while they had the same solid backgrounds, the designer had painted small holiday scenes on the saucer portions. Rachel could only imagine how beautiful they were.

She closed her eyes and squeezed her hands to her chest. This was the find of a lifetime. Rachel did a little victory dance. Seeing it before Owen was only the cherry on top of the teacup sundae.

"Sold!" she cried, pointing to the table.

"What's sold, dear?" a voice asked.

Rachel opened her eyes.

It was gone.

There was a blank space on the table.

"Where did it go?" Rachel demanded.

"Where did what go?" Peggy Zimmer asked. Holiday Beach's postmistress for the last two decades was a stickler for accuracy.

"The blue and gray Prairie Pioneer teacup. It was right there." Rachel pointed at the empty spot, then waved her hand through it in case the cup was still there but had magically turned invisible. She wasn't taking any chances.

"Oh, that nice young man bought it."

There was only one "nice young man" in the building who would have snatched that prize from the hands of victory. The teacup was gone, and Owen was the thief.

"He can't!" It was hers.

"He already did. I know that you were here first, but you didn't say anything. You didn't even approach the table. You just stood in the aisle like some kind of statue."

"I was imagining owning it!"

"But you didn't say you wanted to buy it," Peggy said. "I'm sorry, Rachel. Owen Daye asked if you were interested in it. He even tapped you on the shoulder to get your attention, but you didn't turn around. So I sold it to him."

"Where did he go?"

"He said that it was his last purchase for the day."

This couldn't be happening. Of all the men in all the world to be in the community center that day, he had to be the one to get it. "I don't believe it."

"I wish you'd said something, Rachel, but I can't undo the sale."

"It's not your fault, Peggy. It was mine for waiting so long. I should have pounced on it the second I saw it."

"The good news is that you can still buy it. You know Owen's going to put it up for sale in the shop. Just talk to him and get it before it hits the shelves," Peggy suggested.

"I'm going to do just that." And get *her* teacup back from that no-good, treasure-stealing, arrogant jerk!

CHAPTER 2

OWEN HELD his most recent acquisition above his head as he carefully maneuvered down the narrow aisle lined with breakable lamps and picture frames. He sighed in relief when he reached the small, cleared floorspace at the back of the store where the larger furniture was displayed. The mid-century modern table with its square frame and skinny legs was an almost identical match to one they already had in stock. He was sure the pair would go to the same buyer.

"Pops, Daddy bought a ben table!"

Owen turned to find his four-year-old right behind him. He scooped up the little blond boy and carried him to the front desk. "An end table. Are you helping Pops mind the store?"

"Yep. I made him a picture." Richie pointed behind the cash register, where a variety of crayon drawings on the back of envelopes had transformed the bulletin board into a piece of abstract art.

"That was nice of you. I'm surprised to see you today,

Pops. Shouldn't you be resting?" Owen asked the white-haired man behind the counter.

They both knew the seventy-eight-year-old was supposed to be home with his feet up. Goldie Daye, Owen's grandfather and Richie's great-grandpa, had only recently been given the go-ahead to return to work part-time. This was the fifth day in a row he'd been in the store.

"I did," the sprightly senior said. "Richie helped me with my physiotherapy, then we had a nap, and we only got here about half an hour ago, right, kiddo?"

"Right!"

Behind Goldie, the store's other full-time employee, Blaine Landry, nodded to confirm the story. "Good job on the physio, Pops. Do you want to see what else I picked up today?" Owen asked.

"Did you buy any dinosaurs?" Richie asked.

"Nope, but I got a lava lamp."

"Lamps are boring. I'm going to look for Holly."

"Okay, kiddo."

Goldie helped his great-grandson into his jacket, but left it unzipped, then pulled on his hat and mitts before they let Richie wander around the poorly insulated store-room at the back of the building.

"How was the sale?" Goldie asked.

"Worthwhile. Let me get the rest of it out of the van."

He knew he'd done well that day. Owen had always intended to step into the family business, but not like this. He'd been working as a buyer for a large antique store in Kansas City, gaining experience for when he'd eventually take over Golden Daye Antiques. Then in the summer, Goldie had tumbled down a flight of stairs carrying a chair he had no business carrying. That had landed his grandfather in the hospital for a month. Days after Goldie's accident, Owen's own father had ended up in the same hospital after suffering a heart attack.

Although both men were on the mend now, there had been nobody left to mind the store, so the responsibility to keep things running had suddenly landed on Owen. He quit his job, packed up his house and his son, and move nine hours north to Holiday Beach, Minnesota.

Owen returned with the first load, including the red lava lamp he'd found hidden in a stash of seventies Murano glass, which he'd also grabbed. Goldie rubbed his hands together in glee when as he spread the contents of the boxes around the counter. "Great job, my boy. What other treasures did you find?"

Owen returned a third time with bags full of shelf fillers, as he called them. The snifter sets. The china platter. And the teacup he thought was going to start a riot in the middle of the community center before Rachel Best decided to ignore him completely.

He still wasn't sure what he'd done to annoy the beautiful brunette barista, but she was obviously still upset about it if her behavior at the craft and antique show was anything to go by. Their first couple encounters had been cordial enough, but as summer turned to fall, she'd developed a chill that rivaled the weather, and he had no idea why. "What do you think?"

"Good heavens, Owen, do you know what this is?" Goldie lifted the one-piece set reverently.

"It's a Prairie Pioneer," he replied confidently. Peggy Zimmer had mentioned the name. Aside from that, he knew nothing about the odd little cup.

"It most certainly is. They were only produced for six

years during the Great Depression. There were only a handful to start with. There's a huge market for these."

"No wonder Rachel was so upset to miss out on it." Owen had given her every chance to grab it. He'd even called her name while she'd been doing her statue imitation in the aisle, and only picked it up after she'd ignored him. He hadn't known its provenance; he just knew it was cool and the store's clientele would buy it.

"Rachel Best? Is she doing the teacup thing again this year?" Goldie asked.

"Is she doing what teacup thing?" That was one thing about small-town life that Owen was still getting used to: everyone assuming everybody else knew all the little ins and outs and traditions of the place, even if they'd just arrived.

"Every year Rachel does a fundraiser at Christmastime. She auctions off fancy teacups at her coffee shop. She gets some from the store, but she didn't come in this year..." Goldie's voice trailed off. "Or maybe she tried, and nobody was around to say yes. We've always contributed in the past."

"I haven't seen her or heard from her at all," Owen said. "Maybe she thought since you and Dad were in the hospital, we had enough to deal with. I'm sure she's set up fine for her fundraiser. I know she picked up at least two teacups this morning. One had a butterfly handle."

His grandfather's green eyes brightened at that news. "That's good news. We'll have to make sure we bid on at least one cup to support her this year." Goldie straightened on the stool, grimacing as he stretched his shoulders. "I think that's enough sitting behind the cash register for today," he said.

Owen sprang behind the counter to help his grandfather to his feet. "Do you want me to drive you home?"

"I'll be fine. I'll have another nap before dinner. Can I leave Richie here with you?"

"Of course. He'll be thrilled to help me set up the Christmas displays."

Golden Daye Antiques was late to the Christmas party. They had various festive embellishments up in the store itself—the stained glass suncatcher in the door was primarily red and silver and white—but the paper turkeys and cornucopias on the ottomans in the windows were already two weeks out of date. Black Friday and the days that followed had been a huge weekend for sales with all the tourists who had come into Holiday Beach for the town's annual Thanksgiving weekend events. Then they'd had to restock all the shelves, and before Owen knew it, the calendar had rolled into December. Unless they wanted to jump right into Valentine's decorations, today was the day to deck the halls.

Owen flipped the sign on the door to "closed" after Goldie and Blaine left, leaving him and Richie alone in the shop. He'd anticipated the afternoon's job and had stacked the store's usual decorations into a convenient pile behind the register so he could alternate grabbing green and red ribbons to put between strings of white lights.

But Richie had other ideas.

"No, Daddy, you need this!" The four-year-old disappeared for a moment, then grunted as he hauled an antique crocheted afghan blanket to the front of the store. "See. It's all red for Christmas." Then he was gone again and came back with a red papier-mâché apple.

Owen knew the suggestions weren't going to stop, nor

was his son about to be distracted after specifically being asked to help. Time to direct his attention elsewhere. "Hey, kiddo, do you want to decorate a window?" he asked.

"Okay."

The store had three windows facing Richmond Road: the two main ones, and a smaller one only accessible from behind the counter. "You're in charge of picking everything for the little window."

His son's eyes opened wide in disbelief. "Everything?"

"Everything, but it has to be for Christmas," Owen reminded him. Richie had been concerned that Santa wouldn't be able to find him in their new town. Maybe setting a place for the man in red here would alleviate some of his fears.

It didn't take long for the little boy to become a tiny dictator. Owen hauled a dining room chair with a green upholstered seat and the new end table he'd just put away behind the checkout counter. He draped the afghan over the chair, then set a red tin coffee pot and cottage-shaped novelty teapot on it. A dozen vintage picture books littered the floor around a green-and-cream striped ottoman. The red apple, a framed lakescape in winter, a ship's wheel, and a three-tiered bronze candelabra filled another corner.

Richie put his hands on his hips and surveyed the scene. "This is where Santa rests."

"Is it his library?" Owen asked.

"No, it's his resting spot after work."

"I think it's perfect." Who was he to argue with someone who obviously knew Santa better than he did?

He planned to print a sign for the window that night: "Santa's Resting Spot – designed by Richie, age 4."

A twenty-minute video about garbage trucks on his phone kept Richie occupied while Owen slapped some stuff up in the other window. He couldn't find the tree that traditionally stood in the center of the biggest window, so he left that space clear until he could ask Goldie where it was hidden. The store didn't look especially Christmassy yet, but it was better than nothing. Owen would participate in the holidays for his son, but he wasn't feeling it much the first year after his divorce.

"Daddy, we're having a Christmas party at my new day care this year."

"I know. You told me."

"Are you gonna go to a Christmas party this year?"

"I don't think so."

A little hand slipped into his. "You should. Maybe Santa will bring you an invitation."

"Maybe he will, kiddo."

CHAPTER 3

"AT LEAST THE CAT LOVES ME," Rachel said as she rinsed tuna juice off her fingers.

"That mangy cat loves whoever feeds it."

"That would be me. I told you it was love," Rachel insisted. The first rush at By the Cup was over. The local folks with out-of-town jobs had picked up their morning caffeine fix and headed down the highway. Rachel and her co-barista for the morning, Tina Young, had a twenty-minute lull before the customers who worked in Holiday Beach started lining up. Tina, by virtue of only being the *assistant* manager, was stuck washing mugs and refilling the coffee grinder with espresso beans.

Rachel had ducked into the back to feed her part-time adopted stray who'd been hanging out in the alley behind the coffee shop. The gray cat had been a semi-regular fixture since the summer. She'd managed to get it into a carrier once and took it to the vet for a checkup. It was a healthy female that had not been chipped, so there had been no way to track the owner. Then the stealthy feline escaped the clinic and avoided By the Cup for days. The next time she appeared, Rachel brought out a bowl of water and a tin of salmon to apologize for the trauma; it still took the cat a month to let her get close again.

Holly, as Rachel had named her, was a gray cat with a white face and three white spots on her haunch. The first time she'd shown up, the white bits had been surrounded by splashes of green paint. The green had worn off eventually, but it had looked like leaves surrounding three white holly berries, so the name stuck. "I'm worried that she doesn't have anywhere to stay now that winter's here."

"Rachel, she comes here for food and scritches, and from all the weight she's put on, this isn't her only stop." Tina had already finished with the dishes and was cutting open the bags of roasted coffee beans. They both took a moment to enjoy the aroma waft through the space. "I'll bet she has a home somewhere where her humans are wondering where she goes and why she always comes back smelling like canned fish."

"I can't stop feeding her now. It would be rude." Besides, despite Tina's logic, Rachel didn't think Holly did have a permanent home. Maybe she should look at fixing up some kind of heated shelter for her four-legged friend.

She grabbed the spray bottle and a roll of paper towels and stepped out in front of the counter to wipe down the bistro tables and chairs. The first rush didn't stay long, but the second wave would linger over their breakfast pastries. As she polished the display case, she noticed they'd have to increase their daily order of special holiday pastries—the eggnog pound cake and the gingerbread loaf were almost gone already.

She wasn't surprised. Christmas was a big event in

Holiday Beach. She always put her shop's Christmas decorations up the day after Thanksgiving. Like the other businesses in town, By the Cup had a piece of stained glass on display, in the transom window above the front door. A steaming coffee cup on a counter surrounded by spilled coffee beans was lit from a specially installed light inside. This year, she'd hired the Mackenzie brothers to paint a special scene in the front window: a country sleighride in the style of stained glass. The picture practically begged passersby to come in and warm up with a cup of something hot. She'd manage to frame the window with twinkle lights that had silver tinsel dripping from them. Tina and her other employees grumbled that half of it would end up on the floor, but Rachel loved the way it swayed as the door opened and closed, reflecting the colored bulbs everywhere.

The decorations continued, with the garland framing the pastry case adding a nice holiday sparkle that complimented the gleaming glass shelves behind the counter which would soon be filled with cheerful teacups for the auction later in the month. Eleven good teacups, and a twelfth she had yet to find because of Owen Daye, the good-smelling Prairie Pioneer thief—which reminded her that she needed to get to his store as soon as possible to buy the Prairie Pioneer before somebody else snatched it up.

Tina spoke, breaking her concentration before her internal rant about the handsome, irritating antique hunter could really get rolling. "I think you're obsessing about the cat so that you don't have to obsess about the invitation that came in yesterday's mail."

"I don't think I'm going to Roy and Lucy's Christmas party this year. I barely survived Roy's spiked eggnog last year." That was a lie. Rachel loved the eggnog. It was her solemn declaration to all the attendees after her third one that she'd be bringing a date to the next party—this year's—that set the butterflies loose in her stomach. Her last New Year's resolution to get a social life was a complete bust. It was hard enough to admit without having to show up dateless in front of all her friends again.

"You wouldn't mind the eggnog if you had the right company. It's not too late to find a date Mac mentioned he was going solo this year when he was in here doing the windows," Tina said, referring to the older of the Mackenzie brothers, one of Holiday Beach's most popular bachelors. "Or you could ask Josh Huntington, but if you started dating, that would probably mean going to his gym regularly."

"No man is worth starting a workout routine a month before Christmas, Tina."

"True. How about Mickey Wagner?"

The young, dark-haired hotel owner was a handsome possibility, but she already knew it wouldn't work. "He was my lab partner in high school the year I repeated chemistry. I know way too much about his sports obsessions to even consider dating him."

Tina tapped her finger against her chin. "There's always Owen Daye. He's really cute. He's employed. He drives a nice car. Also, he's new in town. Since he didn't grow up here, you can't know any of his bad habits."

"I know one," Rachel muttered under her breath. What was doubly frustrating was that she'd already considered him. A new bachelor in Holiday Beach was cause for lots of gossip, and after Rachel's first look at him, she hadn't minded listening to all the stories about him. A divorced dad with custody of a young son. He hadn't grown up in town, but he had visited regularly as a kid. He had a head for business and had stepped right up to managing Golden Daye Antiques. On paper, he looked like a catch. In person, however, it was a different story.

Fortunately, the bell over the door jingled, and Tina was distracted by the woman who just entered. "Rachel, I love the new window display. The stained glass look is awesome," Brooke Portman said.

"Thanks, Brooke. I think Mac did a great job," she said in agreement.

"Did you see what Golden Daye Antiques did?"

Rachel breathed deeply, visions of her teacup on display dancing in her head. "No."

"They let little Richie design a window by himself for Christmas. That's what the sign says anyway, and I believe it after meeting the kid. It's definitely a preschooler's version of Santa's library. Lots of green, lots of red, lots of books and toys. And then there's the ship's wheel, because why not," Brooke said.

"I'll have to go take a look," Rachel said, trying not to let her annoyance for the father transfer to what sounded like an adorable effort from his son.

"You can talk to Owen about it at the Chamber of Commerce meeting tonight," Tina said. "You know, use it as an icebreaker."

"About what?"

"A date," Tina tattled.

"Are you interested in Owen?" Brooke asked. "He seems sweet. He came to Aaron's birthday party. Do you think he could steal—"

"—my heart with those amazing green eyes of his?" Rachel finished. "No way."

"I was going to say steal away for a date so close to

Christmas, but yours works too." Brooke winked and grabbed her coffee. "See you next week."

"You noticed that Owen has green eyes, did you?" Tina asked knowingly.

"I'm sorry, I'm much too busy with all the customers to answer questions about my lack of a social life," Rachel said, sticking her tongue out at her friend just before a horde of seniors descended on the counter.

It was close to lunch before she had a chance to pull the first box of teacups from the trunk of her car. Rachel washed and polished them again before she put them and their identifying numbers on the top shelf amid artistically scattered ornaments and bows. She specifically set up the auction to be a simple process because she didn't have time for anything convoluted: people sent their name, cup number, and bid to the store's email. At the end of the weeklong auction, Rachel sorted the emails by cup, and the highest bidder walked away with the teacup filled with the beverage of their choice.

It was a fun event that let Rachel go to various flea markets and antique sales under the guise of "working." With the money going to a good cause, everybody won.

Except when handsome teacup thieves ran away with the prize.

CHAPTER 4

THE RIVER STREET COMMUNITY CENTER showed no sign that only a day and a half ago it had hosted a massive Christmas antique show. It was back to its usual formation of rows of plastic chairs with a single table at the front of the hall. Business owners from Holiday Beach and the surrounding area were mixing and mingling before the board called the Chamber of Commerce meeting to order.

"Yes, we're going to promote Richie to Senior Marketing Vice-president as soon as he wakes up from his nap," Owen joked. His son's window design was a hit, and half the people in the room were offering to hire him. So far, his little entrepreneur had already extorted a cookie fee that afternoon for helping Goldie decorate the tree in the main window. Now Owen had to find a way to explain to his son that he'd had done such a good job that they had to find a new ottoman to replace the one Owen had sold out from under Santa's feet.

Across the room, he saw his grandfather telling the same story to another group. It was good to see Pops circulating around his old friends. His grandpa had been the president of the Chamber of Commerce twenty years earlier and was still active on several committees. He'd taken the summer off for medical reasons, but he was back now and determined to keep giving back to the community.

Josh Huntington called the meeting to order, and people shuffled away from the coffee table to find a seat. "I know folks are putting in extra hours at this time of year, so let's keep this meeting short and sweet," the current president began, and his announcement was immediately met with applause. The board flew through the agenda, including setting up the decoration committee to swap out the business district's Christmas decorations in early January and replace them with the Valentine's Day-themed ones. The last item on Josh's list required came as a surprise. "The board agreed to this last proposal at the eleventh hour, so we didn't have time to warn her. Rachel Best, we passed your Cup of Cheer proposal. Would you like to take the microphone and tell people about your project?"

She pushed a lock of brown hair behind her ear, then took a deep breath. "Hi, everybody. Thanks to Josh and the board for letting me have a minute. As you know, every December I run the Cup of Cheer silent auction to raise money for Main Street United Church Food Bank here in Holiday Beach to help tide them over after the Christmas hamper deliveries. Last year, a few members asked if they could help. This year, the answer is yes. With the support of the Chamber of Commerce, I've opened up the auction to gift baskets from other businesses. Josh is going to put together a list of people who will assist me in collecting donations and running the

expanded auction, so please speak to him if you're interested in volunteering. If you can't volunteer but still want
to help, you can email me at By the Cup to make a
donation."

Beside him, Goldie's hand shot into the air. "We'll
volunteer with the donation collection. Give Owen a call,
Rachel, and he'll be happy to help you," his grandfather
said, offering him up on a silver platter.

"Pops, I don't think she wants to work with me," he
whispered. Every time they'd come face-to-face, it had
been a confrontation.

"We didn't give her a teacup this year. It's the least we
can do," Goldie insisted. "Put us at the top of the list,
Josh," he called out again.

"We've got you down, Goldie. Thanks," Josh said
before he called a close to the meeting.

Owen quickly lost sight of his grandfather as people
mingled and got ready to leave. He was reaching for his
coat when he felt Goldie's hand on his shoulder. "Owen,
you know Rachel Best, don't you? Rachel, this is my
grandson, Owen."

"We've met, Mr. Daye. We were both looking for
teacups at the Christmas craft and antique show this past
weekend," she responded with a tight smile on her lips.

"Owen picked up a few treasures there. He told me
you found a butterfly teacup. I'll bet that one will see lots
of bids." Goldie paused. "I do wish you'd come to see me
directly for a donation this year. You know we would have
loved to participate."

Owen was glad to see her cold shoulder didn't extend
to his grandfather. Rachel patted Goldie's arm. "I did
leave you a couple messages, but with all the changes at
the store this summer, I guess they got overlooked. I'm

very happy to see you back in action, Mr. Daye. I hear I have to come by and check out your holiday window displays."

Goldie beamed. "That was all Owen and little Richie. Obviously, they get their talent from my side of the family."

"Obviously," Rachel agreed.

Without consulting them on their availability, his grandfather proclaimed that Rachel would come over the next morning to help Owen clear out some space in the storeroom for all the donations they were certain to receive. Rachel countered with a better time in the afternoon.

When she looked at him to confirm, she was almost grinning in sympathy as someone who was used to bending to a senior's will. He wondered what it would be like to get a real smile from her.

CHAPTER 5

THE NEXT AFTERNOON, Owen was ringing up a customer's purchase when Rachel slipped in through the front door. She'd arrived early to ensure nobody else purchased the Prairie Pioneer before she had a chance to, but she didn't see it on it any of the shelves in the housewares area. She moved through the fine arts corner and came up empty there too. She was preparing to start a row-to-row search, when Owen approached her holding a massive red latte cup covered in white polka dots.

"It's on the house," Owen said when he handed it to her. "Pops was upset when he realized you didn't contact the store to for our usual donation. Maybe you'll accept this as part of our contribution."

That was strange. And slightly accusatory. "I understand nobody returning my calls with both Goldie and your father being in the hospital, but I also sent a letter asking Golden Daye Antiques if they wanted to participate. I assume you still had somebody going through the mail to pay bills and such. I still didn't get any response.

So please tell your grandpa I didn't forget about him and his previous generosity."

The shocked look on his face seemed genuine. "I don't remember any letter. But the store was in such upheaval when I arrived, it could have accidentally been thrown out. I'm very sorry if it had been. Pops is all about being active in the community but can't do a lot this year, which is why he volunteered me." Owen grabbed a sheet of tissue paper from underneath the counter and gave it a flick.

Unfortunately, he wasn't pay attention to the direction, and the delicate wrapper flapped against the bulletin board and dislodged several of Richie's masterpieces. The rectangular drawings flew across the counter and onto the floor. "Nuts!" he exclaimed.

Rachel scooped up two that landed by her feet, turning them over so she could see the drawings. "Your son has a thing for snowmen," she said as she offered them back, "but it's a clever way to keep him occupied at the counter."

Owen didn't take them. He was staring at the letter in his own hand. The *unopened* letter, she noted, with her name as the return addressee. Owen flipped it to the backside to look at what might be a horse and cowboy according to the hat, then returned to the front. He handed it to her.

"This is the letter I sent," she said after a quick glance.

"I didn't see it. By the looks of it, Richie confiscated it for his artwork before any of us had a chance." Owen slit it open and withdrew a plain sheet of printer paper. Rachel knew what he was reading: best wishes for a fast recovery, and a request for her to come by the store to discuss teacups if Goldie was feeling up to it at a later date.

Rachel pinched her lips together. The whole situation was a dumpster fire. Nobody would benefit if she continued to let it burn. "I guess it's kind of pointless to be mad at the next Picasso simply because he escaped supervision," she said.

"I am really sorry. I didn't realize we hadn't opened your letter before he drew on it—"

"It's not your fault." She gave a little snort. "Okay, it's ninety percent not your fault. At least I know now that you weren't ignoring me on purpose. I *was* starting to wonder." Then she gave Owen a truly friendly smile for the first time. "Can I start over?"

"Sure."

"Hi, I'm Rachel Best, and I own By the Cup. It's a coffee shop on Lakeside Drive. I know you're new to Holiday Beach, but would you like to contribute to my annual fundraiser for the local food bank and donate a teacup to a good cause?" She stuck out her hand.

He gave it a hearty shake. "Hi, Rachel Best. I'm Owen Daye, the new manager for Golden Daye Antiques. My son and I just moved to town, and I'd love to participate in your fundraiser."

"Daddy, why are you holding the lady's hand?" A blond boy raced over to him from the front door.

"We just agreed to work together, so we shook hands to make a deal," Owen explained. He lifted the now-opened letter, but Rachel shook her head, letting him know he didn't have to mention it. Instead, he introduced Rachel to his son Richie.

"Are you going to work here?" Richie said. "Do you know old stuff?"

"No. I work at a coffee shop."

Without warning, Richie pivoted and changed the conversation. "I have a cat."

"I have a cat too. Well, half a cat. She doesn't live with me all the time," Rachel said.

"My cat lives in the store. I'm going to go play with her now." Owen's son didn't even say goodbye before he took off, leaving a trail of dirt and melting snow on the floor.

"That was Richie," Owen said. "On a cookie high, apparently."

"We napped really hard after day care. We needed to refuel," Goldie said, as he stomped the snow off his boots at the front door. "In fact, I could use some caffeinated fuel, so I'm going to run. Rachel, it's lovely to see you again."

"You too, Mr. Daye."

"Are you and Owen all organized?"

"We're just about to start."

Owen ushered Rachel through the store to the large storage room. She heard Richie talking to somebody in one corner, but Owen led her in the other direction and showed her two conveniently empty metal storage units against the far wall. "Will these work?" he asked.

"I think they'll be fine. I can't imagine that we'll get enough to fill all those shelves."

"I think you're underestimating your appeal. I'll bet you a beer at the Escape Room that all these shelves are full to bursting by the time the auction's over."

Owen might be new to Holiday Beach, but that didn't mean he was wrong. Christmas was the season of giving, and Josh had already sent her the names of two businesses wanting to make donations. She was certain the various businesses around town would fall over themselves to be part of the auction. "Bet accepted. I'll happily pay up if I'm wrong."

"While I have you here, I want to apologize about the antique show the other day," Owen said.

She froze. The revelation about her letter going astray had completely shoved their antique show confrontation and her intention of asking for the Prairie Pioneer out of her mind. Owen's apologetic green eyes and his adorable son were dangerous distractions. "Before you say anything, I have to ask a huge favor," she interrupted. "Do you still have the Prairie Pioneer in stock? I want it. Badly."

Before he could respond, there was a crash at the other end of the room. Then one word. "Daddy!"

Rachel didn't have kids, but even she could differentiate between a "come and see" and a "I need help" scream. Owen could too; he was already halfway there before her feet moved.

They found Richie surround by a sea of shattered glass and crockery. The little boy's tear-stained face looked up at them in fear. "Daddy," he cried again. An art piece that was balancing precariously on the edge of an upper shelf trembled at the noise.

Owen strode through the broken shards, shoved the glass sculpture further onto the shelf, then scooped up his son and handed him off to Rachel. She backed away and watched Owen study the scene.

"Are you okay, kiddo?"

"I didn't do it."

"I know you didn't." Rachel could see the little boy couldn't reach that high. "Did you see what happened?" Owen asked gently.

Richie sniffed in her arms. Rachel dug a tissue out of her coat pocket and wiped his nose. "Are you hurt, Richie? Did you get cut?"

"No. Daddy, the cat did it! She was walking on the top shelf and I told her no and I said get down and then she pushed the thing and it crashed and then she got scared and pushed more things off when she ran away." Richie sniffed again.

"I know she's normally good about staying off the shelves, but I also don't usually put light breakables up on them either." He looked around the storeroom. "Richie, do you know where she went? I should make sure she's not cut either."

"She ran away out the window." Rachel guessed it was Owen's steady manner that calmed Richie so quickly. His tears dried, and he twisted in her arms as he took in the shattered glass and china on the floor. "Wow, she really made a mess."

"She sure did. Will you go with Miss Rachel while I sweep it up? I don't want any little boys or cats to cut themselves." He raised his eyebrows to her as he spoke to his son, and she nodded. She could watch a child for a few minutes while he cleaned the disaster zone. Rachel spotted busted wine glass stems, pieces of a large bowl and a pitcher handle, and more broken cups and saucers than she could count, all laying in a puddle of water.

She was glad it wasn't her cleaning up. "My cat likes fish a lot. What does your cat like to eat?" she asked Richie as she took him back into the store.

By the time Owen was finished cleaning, Rachel had to get back to the coffee shop. She was restocking sugar packets when she realized that she'd never received an answer about buying the Prairie Pioneer.

CHAPTER 6

OWEN PRAYED that Richie wouldn't wake up after he tucked him in for the night. He needed some grown-up quiet time to regroup at the end of a busy day.

Decorating Santa's resting spot had calmed his son's worries about Santa Claus finding him in Holiday Beach. Between the store window and the upcoming Christmas party at his day care, Richie was settling into his new home well.

Owen, on the other hand, was still trying to find his place. Making friends as a kid had been a lot easier than trying to do it with the baggage of adulthood and an ex-wife in another state. At least after today, he now had one more friend in Holiday Beach to add to his short list.

He knew things had been hectic and unorganized when he'd first taken over the store; he didn't doubt that Rachel's messages had been lost in the confusion, which was rude enough. But when they hadn't responded to her written invitation, she'd given up on them, and Owen couldn't blame her. Finding the letter while she'd been standing in front of him had been a stroke of luck. He didn't think anything else would have thawed her cold demeanor. But it had, and Richie had worked his usual charm, and all of a sudden working on the food bank fundraiser had become less of a chore and more of an opportunity.

Rachel Best was the exact opposite of the type of woman he was used to. She wasn't quiet or reserved; the energetic barista wore her heart on her sleeve, and her friends and customers all loved her for it. She had a big personality in a small package, and he found it to be a very attractive combination. If nothing else, Rachel could introduce him to a lot of new people through the auction and maybe he could make even more friends in town.

His phone pinged with an incoming message from Roy Wagner. *"Are you the man to talk to about donations, or do I have to go through Josh?"*

"Talk to me. What have you got?" he asked.

"A certificate for a two-hour party in the Escape Room. We're switching it over in January to a new Area 51 theme."

"Sounds great. We'll take it." Owen was shocked the first time he went into Roy's bar and discovered the tiki bar in northern Minnesota had an actual escape room. He'd assumed the themed parties had had their time, but Roy switched out the game every three or four months to keep things fresh, and the patrons kept coming back for more.

"You haven't tried it out yet, have you?"

"Not yet." He didn't know anybody in town he wanted to be locked in a room with.

"Maybe your auction partner could suggest some-body." With a kissy-face emoji.

Owen blinked, then double-checked the sender. It was still Roy.

"*Rachel's cute, right?*" A tiny red heart appeared on the screen.

Bubbles popped up, showing somebody was typing, only for them to disappear and reappear a moment later.

"*Sorry.*"

"*It's Roy.*"

"*Really.*" The texts continued to come quickly.

"*Lucy took my phone.*"

"*She's playing matchmaker again.*"

Owen didn't respond.

"*Anyway, come by to pick up the certificate any evening. It'll be behind the bar. If I'm not there, Emily knows where it is.*"

Owen slowly began to type. "*Is Lucy gone?*"

"*Yes.*"

"*Are you sure?*"

"*Yes. Why?*"

He took a breath. "*Do you think she's right about Rachel?*"

CHAPTER 7

RACHEL DUSTED off the Reserved sign she kept behind the counter and set it on the table in the corner. She didn't use it often, but she and Owen had a lot to cover and a short time to get it done. She was pulling out the stops to make up for her horrendous attitude toward him over the last few months.

"I thought Owen was a rude, teacup-stealing scoundrel who you never wanted to speak to again," Tina said as Rachel prepared for their meeting.

"He is. The teacup-stealing scoundrel part," Rachel clarified. "But he's not rude. My letter asking Golden Daye Antiques for a donation got lost. They literally found it when I was there yesterday afternoon. Then they gave me a great latte mug, so I have my twelve cups of Christmas and can put that part of the auction to bed." It was only a small task on her to-do list but marking it off was one less worry for the future.

"It might be fun to go out with a scoundrel," Tina teased. "Does this mean you've forgiven him for the whole Prairie Pioneer debacle?"

"No. But I might if he promises to sell it to me." The storage room catastrophe had completely distracted her from the teacup conversation, even though she'd specifically showed up early to buy it before it got scooped up by anyone else. Then she'd been too busy today to call. She'd ask Owen tonight to set it aside for her. She was certain he would. "Besides, this isn't a date. It's a business meeting," Rachel insisted. "You'd better not so much as hint otherwise."

Tina put her hand to her chest. "I would never."

"You would always. That's why I'm warning you. We have to get all the donations collected and organized, so please don't make this awkward. We've only just started talking."

"I won't say anything," Tina promised. "Today."

Rachel sighed. "I'll take it."

Owen arrived exactly on time. Rachel got herself a latte and asked what he wanted as he divested himself of his hat, scarf, gloves, and coat. "An apple juice," he requested.

"Nothing hot? We have coffee, tea, hot chocolate, and hot apple cider this month."

"No thanks. Just juice," he said, avoiding her eyes.

She grabbed a bottle from the cooler and her tablet from behind the counter and joined him at the little table. "Let's start with some good news. Josh Huntington emailed me last night. He attached a gift certificate for a two-month membership at Diesel Fitness," she said. Rachel had thought that Holiday Beach was too small for a large gym, but apparently Josh's business appealed to their summer visitors who didn't want to give up their fitness routines.

"That's great," Owen agreed. "You'll be happy to

know that I'm also showing up with a donation. Gaby Boudreau popped into the store today and dropped off a Christmas basket certificate from Butterlicious Bakery. She's offering someone a dozen butter buns, a dozen shortbread cookies, and a dozen cinnamon knots. That should make the winner's Christmas dinner a little easier."

Rachel felt a grin appear on her face. It was beyond her control, but she honestly didn't try to stop it. In a second, she was smiling so hard her cheeks hurt.

Owen leaned back in his chair, giving himself as much distance from her as he could get. "What?" he asked.

"That's a great prize package combination." She giggled in glee. "Buns of steel meet buns of cinnamon." Eat all the goodies, and then work out to make room for more. She hoped Gaby and Josh would find it as funny as she did.

"Goldie didn't warn me about your sense of humor."

"Why would he? His is exactly the same." Rachel always enjoyed working with Mr. Daye. They'd traded jokes and quips every time she'd gone into the store.

"That's why I needed the warning. I've heard the jokes Richie comes home with."

His grandfather's jokes *were* pretty bad. "Fair enough."

They made a list of other businesses that were likely to support the cause, like Taylor Wear for Him and for Her, and the Dew Drop Inn. Owen suggested they ask Flip Flop Fast if the convenience store by the beach would put together a small basket of candy. "It might be better to put it up as a raffle item rather than for auction. Then kids could buy a ticket and have a chance, rather than it just going to an adult with deep pockets."

"I love it," Rachel agreed.

"Also, Roy Wagner contacted me. There's a certificate for two hours in the escape room when their new game theme starts in January."

"Terrific." They really might need all that shelf space after all.

———

They agreed to visit the local hardware store in person. Long before the Chamber of Commerce agreed to get involved, Julie Handler had approached Rachel offering to sponsor something for her auction.

Handler Hardware was one of the businesses in town that was always busy. It was more crowded during the summer, of course, but as the owner like to say, house repairs never stopped. The freshly painted storefront looked small from the front, but it was twice as long as it was wide. The whole building only had five rows, but they stretched out like bowling lanes. Plumbing and electrical supplies each had their own aisle, and the remaining three covered everything else a homeowner would need to make repairs.

Owen and Rachel took their place in line behind Mac Mackenzie. Rachel peeked in Mac's cart of supplies. "Job or house?" she asked.

"All house," the professional house painter confirmed.

"How's the new build coming along?"

"Slowly. I was hoping for more progress today, but I've been behind this woman for fifteen minutes already, and she's still arguing with Julie," he said.

A woman with long black curls that were held in a clip at the base of her neck was tapping a paint card she'd set on the counter. Meanwhile, the harried blonde at the cash register shook her head forcefully. Then the blonde raised her voice, and they could all hear her half of the conversation.

"Handler Hardware is not going to give you a fifty percent discount in exchange for putting our logo on your company's website. I don't know you. I won't sell you products at a loss when you've never been in this store before. I will, however, be happy to ring up your purchases at regular price. You can also register as a contractor and qualify for a discount after hitting the minimum threshold, but that's the only discount I offer." Julie stepped away from the counter and crossed her arms. Rachel had known Julie for years, and even she was intimidated by the Amazon's stance.

"I can get all of this for twenty percent cheaper at a big-box store in Minneapolis," the well-manicured customer insisted.

"Yes, you can. Enjoy the six-hour round trip to get your savings," Julie agreed.

The customer gave a shrill squeak before she stomped to the door. "I'll never shop here again!" she yelled before she pushed on the pull door.

After she made it outside, Julie let loose a huge sigh. "She hasn't shopped here before, so that's not a real loss."

"Who was that?" Rachel asked.

Julie shrugged. "I have no idea. Some city person. I've never seen her before."

"I have," Mac offered. "She's been all over the lot next door."

"The old Shelley's Shack property?" Julie asked as she started scanning Mac's items.

"That's the one," he confirmed. "I know the Piney family was planning on selling it. I guess they did. That woman's been taking measurements and stuff. I waved hello, but she ignored me. I never got her name."

"I'm sure she'll be a lovely neighbor. What's that expression about good fences?" Rachel asked.

"Who needs fences? We'll be best buds in no time." Mac's sarcasm was cutting.

Julie quickly sent Mac on his way, and Owen and Rachel stepped up. "We're here to talk about the Christmas Teacup auction, if you have a minute," Rachel began.

"I only have one. Wait here." Then Julie darted away.

"I'm not sure if that's a good sign or not," Owen said.

Rachel spotted Julie returning lugging a big box. "Let's go with good."

Julie dropped the box on the counter. "What would you think of this for a donation?"

According to the description on the package, it was a large inflatable snowman which was lit from the inside. It would easily be the centerpiece of any house's Christmas yard display. Rachel had broken up more than one coffee klatch when the debate between inflatables versus wire frame sculptures got a little too hot during the town's annual Holiday Decorations Display contest.

"This is amazing! I thought you said that you couldn't keep these things in stock," Rachel said.

"I can't. I'm sold out. But I held this one back just for you. I knew there are several people in town who would be happy to bid on it once I let them know you have it," Julie said.

"You're wonderful," Rachel told her. She was being sincere. "And extra gorgeous today. Aren't you a little overdressed for check out duty?" The tall blonde wore a frilly blouse instead of her normal sweatshirt with the hardware store logo. Giving her a second, harder look, Rachel also noticed that Julie's hair had been styled with care, and she'd put on date makeup instead of work makeup.

"That's why you only get a minute. I'm meeting Lucy's cousin for lunch."

"You're going on a blind date?" Rachel asked in amazement.

"No, Lucy introduced us online. We've been chatting for a while, but Libby's visiting Lucy right now so we're meeting in person for the first time. Wish me luck."

Rachel held up crossed fingers, as did Owen.

"Good luck. Have a nice lunch," Owen said.

"Have a good auction," Julie replied. She handed the box to Owen, then took off her apron and hung it on a hook behind the counter. "I have to run."

Owen watched her leave. "You know, I think she has the right idea."

"Setting something aside for us?" Rachel asked.

"No. Biting the bullet, throwing caution to the wind, and going on a date with somebody new." Owen set the box back on the counter, turned, and looked Rachel straight in the face. "So, what do you say?"

CHAPTER 8

AT FIRST, Rachel didn't respond at all, which was only slightly better than a no. Owen was concerned for a second, wondering if he'd misinterpreted their chemistry. Then, when she smiled at him, the knot in his chest eased.

"I say yes."

"Terrific!"

"What were you thinking?" she asked.

Owen froze. He hadn't planned that far ahead. All he'd thought was that it was the perfect moment to ask Rachel on a date. Now he had to come up with something to do. Dinner and movie? Classic, but boring. It could also be dangerous: if either party decided that their initial attraction was misplaced, they were stuck with the other person for the next three hours. On the other hand, if they really hit it off, they were doomed to sitting beside each other silently, in the dark, when they could be getting to know each other better.

He needed an event that didn't have a set time limit. Someplace where they could do more than sit and stare across a table at each other. Something memorable. As they stepped outside, he saw a poster that answered all his problems.

As part of the town's marketing campaign, they'd started an annual winter kickoff beach party, filled with outdoor events that took place on snow instead of sand. The long list of activities offered some potential date activities. And some things he'd never heard of before, but that sounded like fun. "Do you want to go to the beach with me?"

"Absolutely."

"How's Saturday night?" he asked.

"I'm not on the work schedule, but..." Rachel shrugged, smiling.

He understood. It was one of the perils of being an entrepreneur. Being the boss meant work always came first. "Then barring emergencies, I'll pick you up at six thirty so we can grab something to eat and then get to the party."

"I can't wait."

―――

She didn't wait until the weekend before she contacted him again, although he was surprised it was on the store's landline and not his personal cell phone. "Owen, I keep meaning to ask you and keep getting distracted. I need a favor," she requested.

"Is this the one you mentioned before?"

"Yes. The Prairie Pioneer. I want it. For myself, not for the auction. If you haven't already sold it, can you please hold it for me? Pretty please? I can come over anytime to get it. Any time at all," she stressed.

"I know I haven't sold it. As soon as I hang up, I'll put it behind the counter for you," he promised.

"Perfect. Great. Thank you! You have no idea what this means to me."

"You're welcome."

"I have to get back to work but I also wanted to say that we're going to have a blast on Saturday. The weather is even supposed to cooperate. Can't wait to see you!"

Owen gave his head a shake as he headed toward the china display after her call. He should have thought of setting the Prairie Pioneer aside for her in the first place. Rachel was obviously the person who should have it. He scanned the shelves, but the unique piece didn't jump out at him. He took a harder, second look and still didn't find it. A block of ice formed in his stomach. With all the customers they'd had in over the past few days, it was possible it had been sold, but he didn't remember selling it. He quickly checked with Blaine, but he hadn't sold it either.

"Never mind. I'll check with Goldie," Owen said, refusing to panic over the idea that he might have caused Rachel to miss out on it twice.

His grandfather was in the office, glaring at the monitor and clicking away angrily on the mouse. "Pops, do you remember the Prairie Pioneer teacup I picked up on the weekend?"

"Yes."

"Did you sell it?"

"Sell it? No, not me."

That was good news and bad. "Well, neither did I. And Blaine says he didn't. But I can't find it on the shelves. Do you have any idea where we put it after we unpacked it?" Owen asked. He'd already searched all the usual areas, including the cupboard in the storeroom where they set aside items for pickup. The teacup had simply vanished.

"Why are you looking for it?" Goldie asked.

"Rachel Best asked that we hold it for her. Of course, I said yes."

"It's Christmastime and we're moving stock around daily. I'm sure we'll find it," Goldie continued.

The platitude didn't help. "But now I have to tell her that we don't have it."

"You don't know that. Besides, maybe she'll forget."

"Pops, she almost threw down with me in the middle of the community center for it. Rachel's not just going to forget."

"Don't worry, Owen, it'll turn up."

"That'll take a miracle."

"It is that time of year."

Owen turned the entire store upside down in the days leading up to his date with Rachel. He'd even enlisted Richie, giving him a picture of a similar cup and promising him a prize if the boy found it in some obscure nook or cranny. But nothing had turned up.

Owen arrived at Rachel's small house on Saturday night and wasn't surprised to see the windows completely decked out in white lights, with a real snowman in her front yard. She ran out to meet him and dove into the passenger seat, her long fringed scarf flying behind her. "I've been looking forward to this all week," she said in greeting. "We're going to have so much fun."

"You know, this is my first winter beach party as an adult. I read the poster, but I'm not sure if I'm ready for the experience."

"So long as you're dressed for it. You did dress for it, right?" Rachel asked.

Owen nodded. He wore long johns under his thick jeans and had two pair of socks on in his boots. His wool pullover hid the thin thermal sweater underneath. And his hat and scarf matched his insulated bomber jacket. The only way he could be warmer is if he was carrying around his own furnace.

He finally found a spot to park five blocks up from Lakeside Drive. It wasn't quite seven o'clock, but the streets were already lined with beachgoers and partiers.

"Shall we start with supper?" he asked. Four food trucks had the prime location, parked at the main entrance to the town's sandy public beach. The lines moved quickly, but new people were always replacing the happy customers who were walking away with steaming meat kebobs from Excalibur or fries from the Fry Guys truck.

"Would you like to split a tray of fries with me?" Rachel asked.

"I'd love to."

Owen skipped right over the mayo and vinegar bottles and squirted ketchup into the corner of the cardboard fries container while Rachel brushed snow off a section of picnic table bench. They also grabbed some kebobs, the long skewers alternating chunks of beef or lamb with pieces of bell pepper, onion, and cherry tomatoes.

"I can't believe we ate so fast the food was still hot when we finished," Owen said.

"I can. Fry Guys fries are addicting. I can eat a whole tray by myself, but it's healthier to split it. Not as much fun, but healthier."

"Would you like any dessert?"

"Not yet. Let's work off some of those kebobs. What shall we do first?" she asked. "Oh! I know!" She grabbed his hand and pulled him onto the beach before he could respond.

"Where are we going?"

"To play Snowshoes."

He had no idea what that was, but he quickly learned that was the Holiday Beach winter equivalent of horseshoes, so he had some idea of what was going on. Poor Rachel didn't stand a chance. He'd played every summer for as long as he could remember, either at his grandparents' cottage, or in Goldie's backyard back when his grandfather had owned the large house Owen's father had been raised in.

"You're a ringer," she exclaimed when his sixth neon blue horseshoe hit the metal pole with a clang.

"You never gave me a chance to tell you."

Rachel narrowly avoided getting skunked when one lucky shot gave her three points before he hit eleven, but it didn't take long for Owen to reach twenty-one points to win the game. "If there's ever a partner horseshoes tournament, I want to be on your team," she said as she dragged him over to one of the bonfires further up the beach.

He saw a couple familiar faces huddled around the flames. "Hi, Roy. Hello, Lucy." They'd been the first people he'd met when he'd moved to Holiday Beach. He'd met Lucy Callahan first when he and Richie had stayed at the Dew Drop Inn while they waited for their belongings to arrive. The property maintenance manager met them every afternoon at the hotel's pool for a swim. Then she'd introduced them to her boyfriend Roy Wagner, who owned the bar next to the hotel, and Owen had joined the Escape Room's Thursday night darts league as his first step to meeting new people. It had been a good choice. He hadn't been prepared for Lucy's matchmaking tendencies, although it appeared she knew what she was talking about.

Owen didn't recognize the third person with them, but Lucy immediately provided an introduction. "Owen, Rachel, this is my cousin Libby, who's visiting from Boston."

"Hi, Libby! We've heard about you," Rachel said as she waved her mittened hand.

"How?"

"A certain blonde hardware store owner. How was lunch?" Rachel asked. "Because Julie's a peach."

The pale, auburn-haired woman didn't blink at the implied warning. "She is, and she's meeting us here for supper later. Or now, I should say."

Julie walked over and greeted them all, then stood beside Libby. "Are we eating or what? I've been thinking about lamb kebobs all day."

"We're eating," Libby said, and the two of them shuffled off toward the food truck.

"You're playing matchmaker with them too?" Owen asked Lucy.

"Of course not!"

Owen snickered, and Roy laughed out loud.

"My single cousin is visiting, and I have to work. Why shouldn't I introduce her to some people around town, so she doesn't get bored?"

"Why not, indeed?" Owen echoed, smothering another snicker.

Roy bumped her shoulder. "Come on, Lucy, let's get something hot to eat before I freeze to death."

With the other couple gone, leaving them alone again,

Owen stepped closer to the fire. Rachel got even closer and held her hands over the flame. "This is fun, but I'm freezing. Can we stay here for a couple minutes to defrost?" she asked.

Even through all his layers, he was starting to feel the cold too. "That sounds great." If they fully warmed up, their date could last longer, and Owen realized that he wanted it to. Dinner and a movie would have been a horrible choice for a first date for an outgoing, competitive woman like Rachel, who not only knew how to have fun, but lose gracefully.

"What do you want to do next?" Rachel asked once they were nice and toasty.

"I've already bought you dinner. How about I take you dancing next?" he said.

The pavilion—a large screenless gazebo—hosted a DJ table and two pairs of speakers that broadcast dance tunes into the flat bit of space that separated the beach from Lakeside Drive. Strings of Christmas lights ran from the open-air structure to the light posts around the park.

Owen tilted his head. "Haven't they played 'Rockin' Around the Christmas Tree' already?"

"They play it ever half hour," said a helpful senior who was seated on a nearby bench with a cup of steaming coffee in her hand. "It cycles people off the dance floor and gives them a chance to warm up at the bonfires or try another event."

"That makes sense, Mrs. Wyatt," Rachel said.

"You have good timing. They played the Chicken Dance a couple of songs ago, so it won't come up again tonight."

"Thank goodness for small favors." they said in unison.

Owen held out his hand. "Shall we get this dance started?" he asked as Brenda Lee sang about sentimental feelings.

Their dancing was more swaying than fancy footwork because of their heavy winter boots, but it was still nice. Owen got his groove on doing the Twist; his son had first heard the song at daycare and insisted on dance parties for a week straight. Then Rachel tried to teach him the line dance the DJ put on for that set.

"Right foot, Owen. Right foot forward, then turn. How many right feet do you have?" she asked with a laugh after he ended up face to face with her instead of being pointed in the opposite direction like everybody else.

He tried to turn to face the proper direction and bumped into the woman beside him. "At least three, apparently," he said, apologizing to his dancing neighbor with a grimace.

"Get ready to turn again," Rachel warned him a second after he finally got into the correct position.

"I give up!" He stood in place for the next verse, but he got the hand motions right. By the last verse, he was bobbing and weaving to the beat, but he kept his feet planted firmly on the ground.

"We're going to have to work on that," Rachel announced as she pulled him off the dance floor. "But you have a lot of enthusiasm and energy, so I think we'll be okay."

"I'm game."

Owen was more than willing to get dance lessons from Rachel. He couldn't promise that he'd show much improvement, but he'd give it his all. With enough effort, he might get to be a passable slow dancer, which was terrific incentive if the prize was having Rachel for a partner.

They still hadn't made an entry for the snowman building competition, which would decorate the beach for the rest of the winter, but the idea of sticking his hands into piles of snow made him shiver even more than he already was.

"What do you say we head over to my shop, and I'll fix us each a huge cup of hot chocolate?" Rachel offered.

"No thanks."

"Coffee?" she suggested instead.

"No, really, I'm good."

She gave him a look, and in the dim light, it looked like hurt in her eyes. "You're obviously freezing."

"I am. I think it's dropped another fifteen degrees." The party was set to run till ten o'clock, but a lot of the crowd had cleared out in the last twenty minutes.

"Unless you'd like to say goodnight here and just go home?"

"No, no, I didn't mean that." His brain was partially frozen, but Owen finally understood what he'd said. "I have to tell you something important. When it comes to your offer for hot beverages, the problem isn't you —it's me."

"Are you sure? Because it's feeling a lot like the problem is me."

"I hate coffee!" he blurted out. "Hate it. Hate tea. Hate hot chocolate. I can't stand any drinks that are hot." He paused. "Have I lost your respect forever?"

"Not at all. You just saved me a ton in free refills. I kind of like it," she said. "Why don't we head to By the Cup to warm up at least? I'll have a hot drink like a normal person, and you can chill your own apple juice by holding it."

"That's a deal."

Simply being inside and out of the breeze off the lake was enough to warm them up in no time. By the time Rachel had finished her hot chocolate, they'd both shed their jackets and left puddles of melting snow under their chairs from their boots. He noticed the small teacup display on the shelves when Rachel took her cup to the sink.

"Those are cool!" Four cups and saucers were on the top shelf behind the counter, above a row of coffee bean jars. Owen recognized three of the patterns right away. It took a moment, but eventually he recognized the fourth; Rachel had embellished the design with stick-on gems, adding sparkle and texture to the cup's surface.

"Thanks."

Please don't ask about the Prairie Pioneer, he thought.

"You got a serious look all of a sudden. What are you thinking about?" Rachel asked.

"The Prairie Pioneer."

"You didn't bring it, did you?"

"No. It's still in the shop somewhere."

"Somewhere?"

"It got moved but I'm not quite sure where. We're doing a shelf by shelf search. We definitely haven't sold it, though."

She didn't press the subject. She was too busy yawning. "I'm sorry. I opened this morning so I could have tonight off, and I'm scheduled to open again tomorrow. I have to get home."

She lived close to the shop, so the drive to her place didn't take long. Owen walked her to the door.

"Would you like to come in to warm up again before you go?" she asked. "Your car didn't really have time for the heater to kick in."

"I wouldn't mind, but I'm really just looking for an excuse to kiss you goodnight."

She pointed up. His glance followed her finger, but he didn't see anything in the hanging from the eaves. "What are you showing me?" he asked.

"Invisible mistletoe."

"That'll do." Owen leaned forward and pressed his chilled lips to hers. The contact warmed him instantly. "I can do much better when I'm not freezing," he promised.

"I'll hold you to that after our next date," Rachel said as she laid her hand on the side of his face.

CHAPTER 9

RACHEL TOOK the half-empty can out of the mini-fridge and removed the plastic wrap. The unmistakable scent of fish quickly filled the staff room, but she worried less about the smell and more about the fact that she was holding half a can of tuna. Generally, Holly went through a can every two days, but it had been three days and she'd only been around once.

Rachel had set up a shelter in the alley above her garbage cans. It was as mouse-proof as she could make it, and Holly seemed to take care of the rare rodent who made it through, according to the tufts of fur Rachel occasionally found. When she went to set out the fresh plate of food, she found Holly meowing plaintively from the lid of the garbage bin rather than from the box bolted to the wall above it.

"Aren't you going to jump up for your dinner?" she asked the cat.

Holly snarled, then shifted a bit, which was when Rachel noticed she was favoring her rear left paw. Rachel approached slowly with her hand out. She barely managed to turn the paw when Holly hissed at her and backed away. But Rachel had seen enough. "I'm sorry to say this, but you need to see the vet," she told the cat.

Holly hissed again, as if she understood Rachel. "No carrier this time," Rachel promised. She didn't want to shred her arms again. Besides, Holly was a snuggler. She was certain she could hold the cat in her arms for the trip to the veterinary clinic if she could find somebody else to drive.

Fortunately, she had someone to ask.

"Can you slip away for a couple minutes to drive me to Dr. Miller?" she texted.

"Are you okay? Should I call an ambulance?" was the immediate reply.

She read it twice, then burst out laughing. *"Dr. Miller is the vet, but thanks for the concern."* She snickered again before she resumed typing. *"My sometimes cat has a sore paw. I can hold her but need someone to drive."*

"Sure. Where should I pick you up?"

"Behind the shop."

"8 minutes."

That didn't leave her much time. Rachel moved the tuna can so Holly could reach it, then darted inside to get her coat and purse, hoping there would be enough fish to keep the cat there until she returned. She grabbed a towel from the pile at the back door and crossed her fingers.

Holly had cleaned the bowl bare and was washing her face when Rachel approached. "Want to go for a ride, Queen Holly?" She lay the warm cloth over the cat's back, and scooped her into her arms, taking care to avoid the injured paw. When the cat nudged its head into Rachel's unzipped coat, she chuckled. "I'd be cold too if I couldn't get into my cat bed. I think you'll be spending a few days inside, whether you like it or not. And then we'll find you a permanent home." Holly purred in her arms, so Rachel decided to take it as agreement.

Owen was true to his word. His car stopped at the entrance to the ally that ran behind the coffee shop, and she scurred over to the back door. "Do you need directions?" she asked.

"I looked it up." He did a double-take as she climbed into the back of his car. "Holly?"

"Yes, this is my cat."

"That's also Owen's cat," he said as he began driving toward the clinic. "She doesn't stay with us full-time. We're trying to domesticate her with hugs and treats, but she usually only stays a few days in the storeroom before she runs off again. Now I know who she goes to."

The comment both thrilled and chilled her. Rachel was glad to know that Holly had someone looking after her on the days she couldn't. On the other hand, it sounded like Owen and Richie were providing a home that Holly preferred to hers. Rachel couldn't blame the cat much; she'd prefer a kid who offered endless cuddles and snacks to a lady who stuck to tinned fish and an outdoor shelter.

The clinic was a small building that had been a gas station and garage once upon a time. The bay doors had been sealed and provided a multipaned window that looked into the kennel area. The offices had become treatment and examination rooms, and the lobby was still the lobby, except that instead of motor oil posters, there were pictures of puppies and kittens and reminders to get pets spayed and neutered.

"Lock the door," the receptionist said as they walked

through the front door. "The escape artist has entered the premises."

"Holly's here a little more willingly today," Rachel said. "I don't have an appointment, but she's cut her paw. Can you see her?"

"Do you know what happened?" the vet asked.

"She knocked a bunch of breakables off a shelf in my storeroom. She must have stepped on a shard of something as she hightailed it out of there," Owen told her, and explained how Holly had been splitting her time between their two stores.

Dr. Miller held out her hands. "Let's take a look at Holly. Why don't you two wait out here? And keep that door closed," she warned.

"That sounds like a story," Owen said as they settled in the hard-backed plastic chairs on one wall.

"Let's just say the one time I got Holly here for a checkup, it wasn't voluntary, and she performed a Houdini to end the appointment early. Hopefully, Dr. Miller can do a complete examination this time." Rachel thought about the cat's weight change and crossed her fingers that there wasn't an additional problem with Holly beyond the hurt paw.

Owen leaned back into his chair, then stuck out his legs and crossed them at the ankle. He looked like he was settling in for a long haul. "Do you have to get back to the store?" she asked.

"Now that I know it's Holly, I texted Blaine and told him my lunch hour would be extended due to a cat emergency. It's generally slow right in the early afternoon. He'll be fine on his own for a while." He unzipped his parka. "I had to pull him off Prairie Pioneer search and rescue duty, though. He can't search the storeroom and mind the front at the same time."

"You still haven't been able to locate it?" She didn't understand how it could be so hard to find. It was a teacup. It didn't have legs to run off. It was weird; it had been eluding her from the first time she'd seen it. It was like she wasn't supposed to have it.

"It'll turn up. I'm certain of it," Owen said. "Why are you so determined to get your hands on a Prairie Pioneer, anyway? They aren't common enough that you would have been dreaming of it since you were a little girl. I've been in this business for almost a decade, and I hadn't even heard of them till this month."

"Actually, I have been dreaming of it since I was a little girl," Rachel told him. "Family lore says my great-great grandmother received a Prairie Pioneer and a mini set for Christmas the first year she was married. It was all her husband could afford to give her. It lasted through four generations. But when my mom was little, there was a house fire. My mom burned her hand trying to grab it, but my grandmother dragged her outside. They lost everything in the house except one photo album. I saw a picture of it. It was black and white and blurry, but I saw it. I never thought I'd ever find one for real. Especially in Holiday Beach. Now I have, and I want it, Owen." She leaned closer and stared directly into his eyes. "Badly. Am I clear?"

"Crystal," he agreed with a laugh. "I promise you that you will be the first and only person I think of when I get my hands on a Prairie Pioneer. Pinky swear," he said, offering her his finger.

Rachel shook, and let their linked hands fall between the chairs as they waited.

The analog clock above the reception desk ticked away the seconds, and still they waited. Dr. Miller finally returned with a subdued Holly in a pet carrier. "Is there something else you'd like to tell me?" the vet asked. "Beyond the cut on her foot."

Rachel and Owen looked at each other in confusion. "No?" Rachel answered.

"Your cat is pregnant. Very pregnant," Dr. Miller said. "I expect that she's been scouting locations for a nest. You've told me that she is mostly feral, but the fact that she's comfortable with both of you is promising. I think she'll probably pick one of you as a home base for when she gives birth."

Her visits from Holly had been fewer and further between. "I think she's already chosen Owen's store, but I hope I can get visitation rights," she said.

"Of course," Owen agreed. "We have been seeing a lot more of her lately. She likes our storage room. Lots of nooks and crannies and empty boxes."

"Well, if you keep bribing her with boxes, you'll definitely be the winner," Dr. Miller teased. "If you line a couple with some blankets and keep food and water and a litter box nearby, I think you'll have kittens in a couple weeks."

Holly gave a disgruntled meow and rubbed her face against the wire cage door. The stark white bandage wrapped around her paw had her tilting to one side.

"I think she's ready to get out of the cage. Let's get her home before she really gets angry," Rachel said.

While Owen settled the bill, Rachel crooned to the cat in the box on her lap. She'd enjoyed having a part-time cat, but if it was better for Holly, she was willing to give her up to provide her with a full-time home. She'd miss her, though. Owen and Richie had better be willing to put up with regular visits—especially with kittens in the future.

"Do you want some help getting her settled?" she offered.

"You can't claim half-custody of a cat and then duck out of helping her move. Of course I want you." He blushed and quickly corrected himself. "I mean, your help!"

She wasn't sure which answer warmed her heart more.

CHAPTER 10

OWEN'S MIND raced on the ride back to Golden Daye Antiques. Half the ideas running through his head related to the care and feeding of a half-feral cat who might end up having kittens in his storeroom. The other half were trying to come up with a way to split custody of said half-feral cat, so he'd have a reason to see Rachel every single day.

Fortunately, according to the chatter coming from the backseat where she was talking to the cat, Rachel was all in on the responsibility sharing and was already informing the pregnant puss about her proposed visiting schedule.

"Owen, you know if there are kittens, I'm going to claim at least one, right?" Rachel said.

He glanced at her in the rearview mirror and saw the seriousness in her eyes. "You'll get first pick."

"I might take two."

"Then you might get first and third pick, because I have a sneaking suspicion that Richie will want a kitten from Santa." If they were taking care of one cat, it wouldn't be much of a stretch to get another to keep it company. It would be good for the cats' socialization, as well as for their humans. Richie and Pops both doted on Holly; having at least one in the house would be company for everybody. "I hope that Holly decides to stick around."

"I'm sure she will. I think she's been working up to it for a while." Rachel's generosity of heart seemed to spread to the other back seat passenger; Holly began meowing happily beside her as they pulled up to the store. "It sounds like somebody's excited to be home."

Owen was the most popular exhibit in the store as he carried Holly down the aisle. A busload of Bixby seniors had stopped by the store on their Christmas shopping day in Holiday Beach, and they all wanted to say hello to his cat. When he finally made his escape, he whispered to Rachel, "I should have realized that a cat in an antique store would have been a draw. We should have done this sooner."

The storeroom was still chilly enough to require a coat and gloves. He hadn't worried about it before when there was nothing back here that couldn't freeze. But with kittens on the way, he'd have to do better. Some insulating plastic sheeting over the windows would stop any drafts; moving some boxes and unblocking the heating vents would take care of the rest.

Holly didn't seem to care at the moment. The second he unlatched the carrier door, she took off like a shot, darting between Rachel's legs so quickly that the cat almost knocked her over. "She really doesn't like to be restrained," Rachel said with a laugh.

The pitter-patter of little feet came up behind him. "Daddy, where's Holly? What happened to her?"

"She hurt her paw, but Dr. Miller fixed it. She ran off into the shelves somewhere."

"Don't worry. I'll find her." His little guy was seriously devoted to his cat. His concern and attention cemented Owen's plans to adopt one of Holly's future litter.

It didn't take long for him and Rachel to set a crate near the litter box they'd already bought for Holly. They lined it with the spare emergency blanket from his trunk. The cat would be toasty warm, especially once he finished the repairs.

"Now all we need is the cat," Rachel commented before he could.

Despite Richie's best efforts, he hadn't located Holly after her initial bolt. With his four-year-old checking the bottom shelves, he and Rachel worked their way round the room, searching the upper shelves of the storage units and on top of the large pieces of furniture the store held in the back. "She couldn't have gotten out already, could she?"

"No, I closed the window that she comes through." The tricky cat was in the storeroom somewhere. Owen caught a flash of movement out of the corner of his eye, and then she was gone again. But it had been enough for Richie.

"Up, Daddy. She went up." Richie pointed to the top of a six-tiered unit, the top shelf above even Owen's head.

"Listen, cat, we're trying to help you," he muttered. "Work with me." His fingertips brushed the edge of something cold. The smoothness of it made him pause because it felt like—

"You almost got her, Daddy. Do it again."

Owen went onto his toes and stretched a little further.

There was a brush of fur on the top of his hand. The cool smooth thing he'd felt before moved under his fingertips, and he recognized it as a piece of china. By the time he realized it was the china that was moving and not his hand, he'd missed his chance to grab it. He looked up, saw a saucer teeter on the edge of the shelf, and then watched it fall before he had a chance to react.

He got a pretty good look at it since it flew right by his face. Heavy ceramic. Granite gray cup. Royal blue saucer. A piece of Rachel's heart.

They all shattered when it hit the storeroom's concrete floor.

Owen looked at Rachel, hoping she hadn't seen the falling object. The "O" of her mouth, and the wide-eyed, tearful look on her face said she had.

"I am so sorry," he said. "I had no idea it was up there. I didn't know what it was."

Holly stuck her white face over the edge of the shelf, meowing victoriously. But even the cat fell silent after she saw Rachel.

"I didn't do it, Daddy!"

"I know, kiddo. It was Holly again," Owen replied without looking away from Rachel.

Holly was close enough to the edge that Owen could grab her and pull her into his arms. "I have an important job for you, kiddo. I need you to stick by Holly in her carrier until we get this swept up. We don't want her to cut another paw, right?"

"Right."

Rachel hadn't moved in the time it had taken him to secure the cat and return with a broom. She was speaking now, though. "It's just a thing. Nobody got hurt. That's the important part."

He recognized what she was doing. He'd seen it often in the shop, when a customer's warring ideas of needs and wants clashed, usually over a price tag. But for Rachel, money wasn't the issue. She was trying to talk herself of out wanting the Prairie Pioneer because it was no longer available.

Those conversations never worked. The customer always left disappointed. "I am so sorry," he repeated.

"It's not your fault. It's probably a good thing Holly is going to be staying with you for a few days, though, while I get over her betrayal," she said. "It's okay. I'll be fine."

There was a sheen on her hazel eyes, but he wasn't going to comment on it. She was already devastated; he didn't want her embarrassed as well. "I promise to keep an eye out for another one. We'll hold anything we find for you." It was a weak statement, but it was all he could offer her.

"Thanks." She sounded like he'd just cancelled Christmas. And he felt like a Grinch. "Can you settle Holly by yourself?" she asked. "I think I should head back to By the Cup. Maybe drink a vat of hot chocolate all by myself."

"We can handle Holly from here out, no problem. You take care of yourself."

"Daddy, is that the cup you wanted me to find?" Owen had abandoned his kitty post and was studying the dustpan intently.

"Yes. Holly broke it."

"Can we get a new one?"

Rachel crouched in front of him. "That's a really nice thought, Richie. Those special cups are pretty hard to find, though."

"I'm sure Holly is sorry."

"She's a cat. They always knock stuff off shelves. It's a hazard of having cats. You'll have to shoo her away from anything breakable in the store, okay?"

"I'll watch her extra hard," Richie promised.

"I'm sure you'll do a good job."

She looked so forlorn that Owen pulled her into a hug. Rachel leaned into him. "Don't worry, I'll live," she whispered in his ear. "This just wasn't my year for a holiday miracle. There's always next Christmas, right?"

CHAPTER 11

IN THE FOUR years she'd been in business, there were only two reasons that Rachel had ever closed By the Cup in the middle of the afternoon. One was the day of the plumbing disaster that shall not be named. The other was the afternoon before her annual fundraiser. And today was that day. Like a ship heading into a storm, it was all hands on deck for the USS Cup of Cheer Auction.

Her two junior employees, Caleb Quentin and Jordan Portman, were wiping tabletops and scrubbing windowsills until they shone. Then Jordan went around the shop again, placing a tealight and Christmas candle holder on each table. Rachel didn't keep them out normally, but they added an extra festive touch for the evening.

"How much of the counter do you want me to clear?" Tina asked.

Rachel looked up from her box of Christmas aprons. "All of it. The teacups won't take up much space on their own, but I want them to be separated so people can see what they're bidding on."

She chose a red poinsettia apron for herself. When she held up the other options, Tina grabbed a reindeer with a red pompom nose, Caleb took one that looked like a Santa suit with a big black belt stamped across the middle of it, and Jordan opted for a candy cane print that matched her red and white headband.

Her two newest staff members were the scared kind of nervous, knowing tonight they were carrying part of the weight for an event that was a big deal for By the Cup and the community. Rachel and Tina were the experienced kind of nervous; they knew what needed to be done, and that nobody was going to deliberately set out to ruin the night. It was the possibility of something they hadn't planned for going wrong that had Rachel's stomach in knots.

The coffee shop didn't hold a lot of people, but experience had taught them that tonight they'd be crammed with supporters, so they removed half of the tables and moved two of them in the corner to hold the non-teacup auction prizes. Rachel stepped back to admire the bounty after she rearranged it for the third time.

"It looks great," Tina said. "This will give the food bank a big bump over what we've managed to raise in the last couple years."

"Yes," Rachel agreed. "People really stepped up." She knew Holiday Beach was a terrific place to live, but events like this were physical proof.

"Where do you want this, boss?" Jordan asked. She hoisted a large basket, so filled with candies that only the clear cellophane wrapping kept them from spilling onto the floor.

"Right beside the cash register, please. And make sure you put the ballots, a handful of pens, and the entry jar right beside it." The tickets were only a dollar a piece, but the candy prize had already raised more than anything else in the shop. They'd already had to get a bigger jar to hold all the entries from the kids that had come into the shop with their parents.

A knock on the locked front door revealed another kid. Richie had his face pressed against the lower glass window. Behind him, Goldie and Owen laughed as they juggled packages.

Rachel hurried to let them in. "Thanks for coming early." She directed the men to the prize table, where Owen handed her a recyclable bag brimming with groceries. "What's that?"

Owen adjusted the bag to reveal more of the contents. Rachel could see a box of microwave popcorn packets, two bottles of soda, a bag of chips, and several bags of candy. "It's a last-minute donation from Family Farm Grocery. They're calling it a movie night snack pack."

"We'll take it! That'll buy the food bank at least four bags of groceries." She set it down, then began arranging the new packages.

"I'd be happy to keep an eye on the prizes," Goldie offered.

"I'd appreciate that. It would free up one of my staff," Rachel said while Owen pulled out a chair and angled it into the corner, to give his grandfather a clear view of the room. The older gentlemen sat down heavily. "Caleb, can you please bring Mr. Daye a black coffee?" she called to the young man behind the counter. "Unlike his grandson, he has terrific taste in hot beverages."

Goldie laughed, but Rachel realized Owen's attention had drifted. She followed his gaze to see that Richie had fumbled his way out of his mittens, which were now hanging by strings at the end of his coat sleeves. He shyly dug a dollar bill out of his pocket and held it up to the candy basket at the cash register.

Jordan smiled sweetly at the little boy. "Would you like a ballot, Richie?"

He nodded seriously.

"Okay. Can I fill it out for you?" the teenager asked.

He nodded again.

Jordan carefully printed Richie's name on the ticket. "Are you ready?"

"I'm ready."

The junior barista folded the entry form in half, then dropped it in the jar. Then she gave the jar a shake "for luck."

Richie balled his hands and gave a little shake. "Thank you."

"You're welcome."

Rachel bit back a sigh at the adorable scene. "How upset will he be if he doesn't take that basket home at the end of the night?" she whispered to Owen.

"He's four. He'll be upset for about two days if he remembers that long. He has a Christmas party at day care tomorrow, and I'm sure there will be cookies and candy for days." Owen gave her a reassuring look. "Richie will be fine. He knows that his dollar is buying him a chance to win *and* helping to buy a family a Christmas dinner, and that even if he doesn't win, the family still gets the dinner. That's the main thing."

"Your son has more sense than some adults."

"I'm sure everybody will be on their best behavior tonight. After all, at this time of year, Santa is paying close attention."

The hands on the clock behind the counter moved to

six o'clock. "Look alive, everybody. It's time to get this show started," Rachel announced. She smoothed her apron as she took one last look around the shop. She couldn't spot anything that needed her attention. "Let's have a great night and raise lots of money!"

She twisted the lock and opened the door. To her surprise, a line of people stretched down the block. "Thanks for waiting. Come on, and please be patient with my staff. We weren't expecting so many of you!" She greeted almost everyone by name, and the few she didn't know, her staff seemed to.

She ended up squeezing behind the counter, and saw Owen set Richie beside his grandfather. Then she lost sight of them as she tried to fill orders without getting distracted by the constant pinging of her phone as people texted in more bids on the teacups and prize packs.

She blinked, and suddenly it was five minutes to seven. She finished preparing her final latte, then let loose an ear-piercing whistle to get everyone's attention. "You have a couple more minutes to bid, if you think somebody's got the drop on you. And don't forget about the new movie night snack pack from Family Farm Grocery!" she added, since she hadn't had a chance to add it to the sign in the window.

A couple last-minute bids came in, but for the most part, Rachel was glad to see her inbox fall quiet. She'd already taken care of the emails that she'd received up to four o'clock that afternoon thanks to a nifty spreadsheet from Doug Mackenzie. All she had to do was transfer the stragglers.

She didn't know who placed the French-pressed coffee at her elbow, but she was grateful for it. When she finally looked up, she found Owen looking at her from the far side of the counter. "Hey, no cheating!" she teased.

"I didn't bid. Pops did, but I promised I wouldn't interfere."

"What did he bid on?"

"That red polka-dot latte mug."

"I got that at *your* store," she protested.

"Maybe he just wants a really large cup of coffee for charity."

"Come here." She waited until he leaned closer, then pinched his cheek. "You're too cute."

He leaned further and kissed her cheek. "I know."

A smattering of applause rose from the customers who witnessed the exchange, along with one loud comment of "Hey, no bribing the auctioneer!"

"He is one of the auctioneers, and he can bribe me all he likes," Rachel shouted back. "In fact, I'm letting Owen come behind the counter, and he doesn't even work here."

Owen turned a delightful shade of red at the honor, but he turned and grinned victoriously at the heckler. He joined her in seconds.

"May I have your attention?" Rachel addressed the crowd again. "I think it's time to start announcing some winners from our fourth annual Cup of Cheer Christmas Teacup auction!" Everyone quieted and settled.

She'd done this before, three times in fact, but she still got nervous at the thought that she might mess up somehow. Then she felt Owen's warm hand on her back, and his confidence radiated to her. "Thank you to everybody who participated in this year's fundraiser. Whether or not you win, we appreciate your support. Let's start with the first six teacups."

One by one, Rachel called out the name of the highest

bidder. The amounts varied from prize to prize, some teacups garnering more interest than others, but she handed over the teacup with thanks, and Caleb or Jordan filled it with the winner's beverage of choice. They hit five hundred dollars at the halfway mark.

"Do you want to do the auction prizes?" Rachel made the offer to Owen for two reasons. He'd done the lion's share in gathering, wrapping, and organizing the prizes, so she wanted him to get the credit, especially since he was relatively new to the community. Everybody knew his grandfather, but with Owen taking over the store, she wanted him to have the chance to be known for himself.

The less altruistic side of her simply wanted to be able to share the experience with him. The fundraiser had been hers. She'd done some thinking over the last week, and if Owen wanted to make it *theirs*, she was willing to share it with him in the future.

"Sure," he agreed.

He was taller than she was, but he had to work harder to get everyone's attention, so she whistled for him. "We have some new contributors to this year's fundraiser," Owen said, "so I'd like to thank Taylor Wear for Him and Her, Handler Hardware, Butterlicious Bakery, Diesel Fitness, the Dew Drop Inn, Family Farm Grocery, the Escape Room, and Flip Flop Fast for their donations. Now it's time to announce those winners."

It stung her pride a little that Julie's Christmas lawn decoration blew away the highest teacup bid by more than double, but the money was going to a good cause. And Rachel had seen the other bids. The winner, a local tow truck driver, had bid a hundred dollars more than the next highest bidder.

"Thanks," Tom Latt said as Owen handed over the

box. "We really wanted this for our yard. You've made our Christmas!"

Rachel and Owen had a vigorous debate about whether or not to do the candy basket next. She wanted to save it to the end simply due to the huge number of entries. Owen had countered with the argument that most of the entrants had a bedtime that was rapidly approaching. As someone who was a parent, he probably had a point, so she conceded.

As Owen made the announcement, Rachel lifted the light plastic jar off the counter. She pushed up her sleeve and stuck her hand into the paper ballots, stirring them well. She pulled out a single sheet, then unfolded it carefully. "Congratulations to... Shelly Pham! Is she here tonight?"

An excited mitten waved in the air, and Rachel handed over the overflowing basket to a six-year-old girl who drooled over the prize pack, seemingly deaf to the words of her mother behind her.

"Shelly, that basket of candy will last you till Christmas. You will not get to eat it all this weekend. Shelly, are you listening to me?" the girl's mother asked.

"Good luck with that, Helen," Owen said. "I'm glad I'm not having that conversation with Richie." The crowd got a good laugh at that, and then thinned considerably as all the parents and candy basket entrants headed out.

"Now we're back to the teacups," Rachel announced. "We have six more cups to go to make a very merry Christmas for a lot of families in the area."

"Seven," Owen corrected her.

"Seven what?"

"Seven teacups," he said.

CHAPTER 12

RACHEL CERTAINLY WAS MAKING his first Christmas in Holiday Beach memorable. Both she and Goldie had referred to this as a "little" fundraiser. By the Cup was so packed that Owen was thankful to be squished behind the serving counter with only four other people. Folks had turned out in droves to help the local food bank and the businesses that were supporting it. He'd enjoyed his old neighborhood in Kansas City, but Holiday Beach was a place working together on a town-wide scale to help the whole community. He was grateful Rachel had given him a chance to be part of it.

He was extra grateful that he had a way to say thank you.

Rachel held up her hand to the crowd. "What do you mean, seven?" she whispered.

"Trust me."

"I don't have any bids. Or an auctioneer to do it live. Or a seventh cup to auction off, which is a bit of a problem, Owen!" By the end she forgot she was supposed to be whispering, but she missed the smirks from the people behind her.

"Rachel, it'll be okay. I have a plan," he said. A plan put in motion by his grandfather, which Owen had finessed in order to ensure it got the results he wanted. "I'll take care of the auction part."

"You'd better. Don't think I won't throw you under Santa's sleigh if you don't follow through."

It was all he could do to keep a victorious grin off his face.

Cups seven through eleven happily went to their new owners. There was some good-natured ribbing between the Zimmer twins, who had gone after the same cup with vigorous bidding.

Rachel grinned after she announced the winner of the twelfth cup. Ashley Shott, the winner, adamantly insisted that she did not want the beverage that accompanied the prize. "I can't risk washing it and having any of the sequins come off," Ashley said. "My class is doing a reading challenge for historical books, and this will be a great prize from some pretend royal court."

"I hope your students enjoy it," Rachel said, carefully protecting the cup with bubble wrap and putting it in a gift bag for the teacher from the elementary school.

Owen watched Rachel take in the happy faces in the crowd, and the empty shelves along the wall. Her smile was full of happiness and goodwill for the season; nobody could doubt that. But the way she stood, and the bags under her eyes, and the way she kept smothering yawns and hiding them behind mugs as she sipped coffee told another story. The announcement of the winners itself had only taken a little more than two hours. The entire event had taken a year for her to put together. She needed some downtime to recover.

Fortunately, what he had planned wouldn't take very long.

"Okay, Owen, you're up. Do not mess up my auction or else," she told him.

He wasn't sure whether or not she was kidding. He cleared his throat. "Thanks for staying for the surprise auction item, everybody. As you know, Rachel Best has been planning this event for a year, and she's done a great job. But there is one flaw in her system."

He heard a mock-outraged gasp beside him. "Are you saying I'm flawed?"

"I'm saying there is an unavoidable weak point in your setup," he continued.

She crossed her arms. "Please, enlighten me."

"You yourself can't bid on any of your prize packs. In order to be scrupulously fair, you have to take yourself out of the running. And I, and everybody else here, know you love a good teacup."

"He's not lying," Peggy Zimmer yelled. "I saw you almost take him down for a butterfly cup earlier this month."

"Do you blame me? Jean Wyatt paid a lot of money for it. How could I keep it and deprive her of the chance to worry about breaking the handle every time she wants a cup of Earl Grey?" Rachel shouted back.

She turned back to him and smiled at him to keep going. He was grateful to see the hesitation in her eyes when he'd begun to speak had turned to curiosity. "As the new partner in this little enterprise, Golden Daye Antiques is providing a mystery teacup to bid on. But only *you* are allowed to bid on it, and it's a surprise. Blind bid only. You only get to see it after you've paid up."

Rachel's eyes widened, and her jaw dropped. "What are you talking about? It can't be the Prairie Pioneer. We both know Holly smashed it to bits."

"It's true. Sadly, that cup was destroyed. This is something else."

"What is it?"

"Do the words "mystery," "surprise," and "blind bid" have no meaning for you?" he teased. "Are you game?"

"Of course! As owner of By the Cup, I bid twenty dollars for the mystery auction item."

"So—"

"Wait!" Rachel whipped off her poinsettia apron and raced around the customer side of the counter. "As a private citizen, I would like to counter that bid at forty dollars."

"Okay, going once, going—"

"Wait!" Owen facepalmed as Rachel came back and snatched her apron from the counter. "Forty-five dollars! Wait!" He didn't even try to speak as she ran back to the hole in the crowd that she made the first time. "Fifty!"

He waited. "Is that your final bid, Private Citizen Best?" he finally asked after she stayed silent for an entire fifteen seconds.

"It is."

"Does By the Cup Owner Best wish to counter-bid?"

"Nope, that's her limit too," Rachel responded to much laughter.

"Fine then. If both of you are absolutely certain." He waited one more time, then quickly said, "Sold to Rachel Best for fifty dollars, one mystery prize!"

Rachel pulled fifty dollars from her wallet and

pushed them across the counter to Owen. Then she made grabby hands. "Gimme!"

"First, I'm going to match your bid." He set his own money on the counter. Then he gave Tina a wave, and Rachel's assistant manager ran into the back room and reappeared a moment later with a gift box.

"Show us, Rachel," Poppy Zimmer called.

"I'm working on it. He used a lot of tape," she mumbled.

She wasn't kidding. He'd sealed the small, four-inch square box with tape and Mylar wrapping paper, which was next to impossible to tear. Rachel was motivated though. In under a minute, she had the wrapping paper off and was peeling back the lid. "Oh, my gosh. Owen!" Then she fell silent.

"What is it, for heaven's sake?" Peggy Zimmer demanded.

All Rachel could do was shake her head, her eyes never moving from the box.

"The Prairie Pioneer teacup from the antique show is truly a goner. Death by cat," Owen said. "I knew Rachel really wanted it, and I felt horrible that not only had I bought it out from under her, but that I couldn't sell it to her either. So, I did a little research and found something I hope is almost as good."

"It's as good. Trust me. Better even," Rachel said. She dipped the tips of her forefinger and thumb inside and pulled out a small cup and saucer set that formed one tiny unit. "Owen, it's exquisite."

Delicate evergreen boughs circled the saucer, with a detailed brown pinecone under the handle. On the cup itself, a cardinal sat on a low branch while another curved over its head. The brilliant red of the feathers and the fresh green of the boughs jumped off the white background. Although it displayed none of the traditional hallmarks of the holiday, it couldn't be anything but a Christmas cup.

"Look, the hook ring is still intact," Rachel breathed in wonder, as she pointed out a bump in the clay with a hole no thicker than a darning needle above the tiny handle. "You thread that with a ribbon so you can hang it on your Christmas tree." She turned it over in her hands again. "Owen, it's beautiful. It's absolutely perfect."

"You can thank me later," he said.

"I'll thank you now." She rewrapped the delicate ornament in the bubble wrap, returned it to its box, and carefully tucked the whole package under the countertop. Then she took his face in her hands and kissed him soundly in front of everybody in the coffee shop.

Owen didn't mind a bit. He also didn't mind the cheering coming from their audience. He didn't even mind the fact that she tasted like coffee. In fact, he was starting to like it.

"I think Rachel got the best lot of them all," Poppy Zimmer said.

Rachel finally let him go. "I think I did too."

"Are there any last-minute announcements you need to make?" Owen asked. He wanted to get her out of there to discuss that had nothing to do with teacups or auctions. Like kisses and future dates and plans for the holidays.

"I think we've given them enough of a show. Thank you very much, everybody for all the support you've shown for the Main Street United Church food bank. Congratulations to the winners. As for the rest of you, please feel free to come back to buy a cup of coffee or visit any of our sponsoring businesses to buy your own prizes.

Have a good night, everybody, and if I don't see you before the new year, have a very merry Christmas wherever you are."

Calls of good night and Christmas wishes flew around the coffee shop as the exodus began. Owen stepped out of the way to make room for the last-minute customers who wanted a drink for the road. Since his grandfather had left with Richie after the candy basket draw, he took a seat in the corner and waited for the place to empty. He was exhausted; he could only imagine how tired the rest of them were.

Forty-five minutes later, all the staff was gone, and he was alone with Rachel as she locked the front door. "Five thirty is going to come much too early, but I'm too wired to sleep. Would you like to come over while I have some hot chocolate and try to relax? I have juice boxes," she said.

"Juice boxes? I'm there."

She abandoned him as soon as they stepped through her front door. By the time he'd removed his boots and coat, she was back, a little plastic container in hand. "It's my sewing kit," she explained. "I'm not going to waste a second in getting my new little beauty on the tree."

She patted the sofa seat beside her. As he held the needle and scissors and whatever else she handed him, Owen began to understand the depth of her appreciation for his gift. "Now we've got a Prairie Pioneer back in the family. I'm going to show it off to my mom when she comes over on Christmas Day." She closed one eye and pressed the thread through the tiny hook on the first try. "But I want you to be here when I hang it on the tree."

She had a skinny, artificial tree but it had a place of prominence in front of her window. Strings of lights shone through the branches that were heavily laden with silver strands of tinsel. Rachel shifted four ornaments to give Owen's teacup a place of honor in the middle of the tree. He noticed that Rachel hadn't gone with a theme; no two ornaments were the same. Instead, the tree was a riot of color united only by the small white bulbs that illuminated all the decorations. A stained glass sea turtle, which looked more like a suncatcher than an ornament, caught his eye. "Is that a Christmas turtle?" he asked.

"No, that's a souvenir from the time I spent my Christmas vacation in Cancun with my college girlfriends. I nearly drowned myself trying to learn how to snorkel, but it was worth it." She pointed to a mercury glass seahorse beside it. "That was a different trip. From when my family went to the aquarium in San Diego when I was in high school."

"Are all of these ornaments from various trips?" he asked, amazed to see so much of her life on a Christmas tree.

"Most of them. Some are gifts from friends. Like yours. Those ones are extra special."

He joined her at the tree. She hadn't turned on the overhead lights in the living room, leaving only the tree and a few candles to brighten the room. "I think you're extra special." They may have gotten off to a rocky start, but Rachel was the best thing that had happened to him in Holiday Beach. He wanted her to know that.

"You've admired my Christmas tree, but you haven't said a word about my mistletoe."

He looked around the room but didn't spot any of the greenery hanging from a doorframe or even pinned to a lamp shade. "I didn't see it."

"Of course not. It's invisible, remember?" she reminded him.

Owen loved that she could tease him like that, even though they were still getting to know each other. They'd gone from enemies to friends to this in less than a month. But it felt right, and it seemed like Santa was helping things along. A Prairie Pioneer mini coming onto the market the day he decided to look for one. Holly the cat providing some common ground with Rachel and his son. The auction for introducing them as a couple to the community. He couldn't have planned it better if he'd tried. "Well, in that case, we'll have to use our imagination."

Her peppermint mocha kiss was addictive, but he stepped away after a moment. "There's something I've been meaning to ask you, and since you're feeling grateful, this is a good time to ask."

"Probably," she agreed, her hazel eyes shining in the candlelight.

"I've been invited to Roy and Lucy's Christmas party at the Escape Room. Are you going?" he began.

"Yes. The only question is whether or not I'll have a date."

"You will. Did you know they've challenged us to a karaoke contest?"

"Not on your life, Owen Daye."

"What if I promise that you'll find some extra special coffee beans in your stocking on Christmas morning that will go with your new teacup?" He wasn't above bribery to convince her to say yes.

Rachel smiled, then crooked her finger into the V-neck of his sweater and pulled him closer. "I think you and the mistletoe might convince me."

EPILOGUE

"Nope. Nope. I'm still not convinced. I am not singing in public. I refuse." Rachel crossed her arms over her cranberry red sweater and dared Owen to say something. Despite his bribery and kisses—she'd almost weakened that evening at her apartment after the auction—she'd stood firm and he hadn't insisted she sing with him.

Now it was the evening before the day before the night before Christmas, and the Escape Room was closed to the public. The owner Roy Wagner, his brother and co-owner Mickey, and Roy's girlfriend Lucy Callahan were hosting the private event for a few friends. But since Mickey and Roy had grown up in Holiday Beach, and Lucy had never met a stranger in the year she'd been living there, the bar was almost as crowded as it would be on a normal night.

Pool balls cracked against each other in the far corner, while Sheriff Aaron Gillespie and his girlfriend Brooke Portman finished a duet on the makeshift stage across the room. The wild applause after their rendition of

"Walking in a Winter Wonderland" put them in the lead for most popular singers of the night.

Mac Mackenzie was up next. "This song is dedicated to my new neighbor, Lorelei Baker," he informed the audience. Then he broke into a hilarious version of "I'm Getting Nuttin' for Christmas."

Owen wrapped his arm around her shoulders. "Come on, Rachel, we can beat Mac. What's the worst that could happen?"

He was persistent, but Rachel didn't sing in public. "Terminal embarrassment! Owen, I don't sing. Not karaoke, not with a group around a campfire, not even alone in the shower. I just don't."

Her boyfriend sighed but nodded his acknowledgment of her answer. As he walked off to get her another eggnog, she offered a compromise, whistling to get his attention. "I may not sing, but I can whistle counterpoint to your melody if you'd want to try that."

Owen nodded eagerly, and almost pushed Mac off the stage to be next. Since it was Christmas karaoke, she was certain she'd be able to keep up with any song he picked, but she was especially pleased when he chose "I'll Be Home for Christmas." Bing Crosby had done a version with a twittering whistled melody, and she did her best to emulate him.

They finished with more applause than Mac had received, which meant they wouldn't come in dead last.

"I think that's against the rules. Rachel didn't actually sing. I think that should disqualify you," Mac complained over his beer.

"You're channeling Scrooge tonight? What's wrong? More trouble from the architect next door?" Owen asked.

The architect they'd run into at Handler Hardware had made similar impressions at every business in town.

The reigning king and queen of the jukebox joined them. "Don't tell me your neighbors are blocking your driveway with equipment again," Brooke said in sympathy.

"Not at all. Now they're pulling up my driveway and dropping their loads in the middle of my property. Apparently, Ms. Baker told them the lot was unused and available for storage."

Rachel outright gasped. "What did you do?"

"I had Aaron haul the stuff away as lost property. It's sitting in the police impound lot right now," Mac told them with a grin.

"So, you are a Scrooge, but a justified one," Owen amended.

"These days it may sound petty, but I'm living for the humbug," Mac agreed. "I keep hoping that Lorelei Baker is a ghost in a bad dream, and she'll be gone when I wake up."

"I don't think you'll be getting that Christmas miracle," Rachel informed him.

"Santa may come through for me yet," Mac said, crossing his fingers.

As other friends joined them, more horror stories about the build beside Mac's got shared. But when Owen stepped away to take a call, and his face turned white after he answered his cell, Rachel lost all interest. She excused herself and made her way to the quiet spot he'd been able to find.

"What's wrong?" she mouthed.

He nodded to acknowledge her but kept all his attention on the conversation. "Is he alright?" Owen asked the caller. He listened for a moment. "No. I don't think we need to call Dr. Miller until the morning. Yes, we can come home now. I don't think Rachel will mind if we leave early. See you soon, Pops."

"What's wrong?" she asked again. "Is Richie sick?"

"Richie's fine. Holly, however, is now the proud mama of four Christmas kittens."

"Your house is going to be a madhouse for the next couple of months," Rachel said with a laugh.

"But I'll have you around to help, right?" He looked at her. "I will have you around, won't I, Rachel?"

"Of course! We're Christmas kitten grandparents now. We have joint custody."

He looked up and pulled her closer. "I had to make sure we were under the mistletoe." He kissed her. "Merry Christmas, Rachel."

"Merry Christmas, Owen."

THE END

PART TWO

SWEET CHRISTMAS

Love is in the air at Butterlicious Bakery, and Santa may bring a second chance to two star-crossed sweethearts. Firefighter Devon Sparks had to leave town on the job just when things with baker owner Gaby Boudreau were heating up. Now he's back at the starting line and he hopes that, with a little help from his hands and some holiday spirit, he'll be able to pick things up and deliver a merry Christmas to the woman of his dreams.

CHAPTER 1

GABY BOUDREAU HAD RISEN before the sun. It sounded a lot more impressive than it really was. Early mornings were mandatory for bakers, and since it was December in Minnesota, the sun didn't come up till well after seven anyway. Butterlicious Bakery had customers who were awake and on the go long before then.

She'd already popped a set of trays into her enormous commercial ovens and was filling a bowl with ingredients for her Christmas cookie of the day when the bell over the door jingled. Gaby glanced at the clock on the wall and knew who it was before she walked out to the front of her shop. He was right on time.

"Hey, Devon," she called, aiming for casual and trying to hide her curiosity at what he had planned next. Because this was no ordinary customer.

The stocky firefighter's brown eyes were the only things visible between the brim of his ski cap and the upper edge of his scarf. The twinkles she saw in them told her Devon was up to something. "Good morning, Gaby. What's on the menu today?"

"Muffins in about twelve minutes. I made cranberry bran this morning."

"I like cranberries," Devon said.

*

Devon Sparks liked everything about Gabriella Boudreau. The long, thin black braids she wore down her back. The way she lived for bright colors like the fuchsia top she wore under her apron. Her passion for celebrating every holiday with a delicious, tasty treat. That last one was a big one. The woman was an artist in the kitchen. He held Gaby personally responsible for adding an extra mile to his daily runs. He visited the Butterlicious Bakery nearly every morning, and it hadn't taken long to become evident at his waistline. It was a price he was willing to pay. He scooped a handful of red and white mini-cookies out of the sample basket.

"Want to wait?" she asked.

He smiled when he realized she was reaching for a coffee cup even as she asked the question. It was progress. Finally.

He tugged off his ski cap, exposing his dark, shaved head to the elements. The bakery was warm all year round, but in December, he especially appreciated the heat from the kitchen giving him a chance to warm up before he started his drive to the fire hall in Bixby. Since Holiday Beach didn't have its own hospital or fire department, Devon was grateful to get a job in the neighboring town. The drive was just long enough for him to eat one muffin if he paced himself, but he always got two because they tasted so good.

"Yes, please." He strained to look over the display case and into the bowl on the back counter. "What's the cookie flavor of the day?"

"Hot chocolate cookies with a fudge-y center."

"What's the fudge of the day?" he asked.

"It's like you *want* Santa to leave coal in your stocking," she retorted.

Devon was well aware that the bakery had offered a fudge-garnished sweet every day for the last week and a half. At first, he thought it was a time-limited special. Then he accidentally discovered the real reason behind it. One that Gaby did not want to talk about.

He heard the coffee slosh against the lid on his cup as she slammed it down on the counter. Her brown eyes blazed as she told him off. "I am beating this fudge recipe, Devon. I don't care if it takes me till Christmas." He knew the exact instant she realized that she'd dropped her guard when she gave her head a shake and offered him a professional smile. "Don't worry about me. I'm also making gingerbread for today's special."

"Sounds great."

He sipped carefully as he watched Gaby sneak glimpses at him. She twisted her hands around her coffee mug. Only a baker would have one that said, "Admit it—you love my buns."

"How's your grand romance coming along?" she asked.

"Slowly." Much too slowly. He could even say a glacial pace would be an improvement. Especially since Gaby was the one he was supposed to be romancing.

He'd had a great time with Gaby when he had taken her out in the spring on two amazing dates. But then the world had conspired against them, and everything had fallen apart.

Devon had been prepared to go a couple of months without seeing Gaby when he took a job fighting forest fires in the northwest. The plan had been to keep in touch, but that hadn't lasted long. First, he'd lost his phone in the middle of nowhere. It had taken him a week to get a replacement. Then he'd been too busy and tired to text. The two of them had lost all momentum by the time he returned to Holiday Beach. Then Gaby got busy with her bakery over the busy summer tourist season. One month had rolled into another, and he didn't know what to do to stop the drift.

It had taken some time for Devon to come up with a plan and even longer to get it in place. But now, he was trying to reignite the flame they'd once had.

At the beginning of December, he'd put on a show in the middle of Butterlicious Bakery, leaving a message on his own voicemail, saying he had no clue what to get "her" for Christmas. Gaby asked him what the problem was and volunteered to help.

Well, "volunteered" might be too strong of a word. It was more like she was recruited by Poppy Zimmer, the secretary at the police station and one of Holiday Beach's busiest bodies. He'd arranged for Poppy to be in the bakery during his performance, and she'd been more than happy to assist with some matchmaking on his behalf.

"I'm trying to find the perfect Christmas present for a woman I really like. What do you think? Jewelry?" he'd asked.

"How long have you been dating?" Gaby had asked.

"We've only gone out twice, but I really like her."

"No jewelry. It's too soon," Poppy had commented definitively.

He glared at her since she was supposed to be help-ing. *Well, there went that idea.* It's not like he'd been thinking of a ring or anything.

"What does she like? What are her hobbies?" Gaby had continued.

"She likes to entertain," Devon had said. He knew Gaby was a foodie who experimented and loved to share the wealth with her friends. She was even more social than he was.

Her eyes lit up. "That's promising. She'll probably be doing something for the holidays, right?"

"I know she is." He'd overheard Roy Wagner and Lucy Callahan talking about Gaby's upcoming holiday open house when he'd been in the Escape Room the previous Friday night.

"Get her something festive that she can put out when people come over. Something decorative," Gaby had suggested.

Festive? Decorative? He was a single guy. The decorations in his apartment consisted of a framed football jersey and a painting his father had given him as a house-warming present when he'd moved out. "Like a poinsettia?"

Gaby had looked at him in horror. "If she's your grandma."

Poppy had snorted. "Get something pretty she can show off. That way, every time she hears someone compliment it, she'll think of you," the other woman had suggested.

It was good advice. The windows of Butterlicious Bakery looked festive, and people commented on them all the time. He assumed Gaby was all about the holidays at home too. Unfortunately, he didn't have a clue as to which kind of decoration to get. He needed help. Fortunately, he knew a guy. "Thanks. I'll do that."

That had been a week ago, and he was still without an

idea. This morning Devon dug a little deeper. "Do you know anything about wine?" he asked as he waited for the promised muffins.

"I know what I like."

"I need suggestions."

"For a date with your mystery girl?" Gaby asked.

"Jealous?"

"No."

The kicker was that she *didn't* sound jealous. And Devon wanted her to be. What was it going to take? "Come on, Gaby, help me out. What kind of wine do you like?"

"Me? I like a Moscato. It helps me to stay sweet and bubbly."

"You are that." She was adorable when she blushed. He didn't get to enjoy it for long. After that exchange, she ran and hid in the kitchen, her braids bouncing as she moved.

While he waited for her to reappear, Devon looked around the bakery. It had gleaming chrome and stainless-steel fixtures, warm wood trim, and just enough red to give the place some color. Normally. Ever since the calendar page flipped to December, Gaby added a new ornament or decoration to her shop every single day. Today it was a snowman snow globe on her counter. She'd also taped a length of garland around the sign that had her hours.

A minute later, he heard an oven timer ding, and she returned to the front to hand him a bag with two piping hot muffins, no butter, just the way he liked them.

"Thank you."

She gave him a small smile and a shrug.

"Gaby?"

"Yes?"

"I'll see you tomorrow."

"You know where to find me.'

CHAPTER 2

YOU KNOW where to find me? Why didn't she just say, "When you get around to it, I'll be here if you want to ask me out again?" Gaby preferred to think she had a little more finesse than that.

They had gone on two dates in April, and then Devon had disappeared. To be fair, he'd gone to fight forest fires in Montana and then come home to have a family emergency waiting, so she hadn't had a chance to see him. That had rolled into her expanding the bakery's staff and hours over the summer. She hadn't had time to think about Devon, let alone wonder what he was doing. But lately, he'd started coming around again, and she wanted to know what he was up to. Because it was entertaining.

When she didn't immediately fall at the firefighter's feet when he reappeared, he got serious and started to work for it. It was killing her, but Gaby pretended not to notice their "random" encounters in town or the winks from the mutual friends who ducked into doorways and down aisles after they played their parts in arranging the set-ups. At first, it had been fun, but it was time for Devon to get to the point.

With the holiday entertaining season gearing up, Gaby took advantage of a quiet afternoon and closed early to run some very necessary errands at Riesling and Brie, Holiday Beach's premier—and only—wine and cheese shop. The small store catered mostly to tourists during the summer, but they always did good business when the locals had something to celebrate

Gaby grabbed two bottles of red wine to use as future hostess presents, then swung down the white wine aisle on her way to the check-out stand. She froze in front of an empty shelf.

"Now, Gaby, don't panic," a calm voice said from behind her.

"Megan, where's my Moscato?" Gaby asked in shock.

"We sold it."

"But it's *my* Moscato. You order it for *me*."

The deeply tanned store owner laughed at her. "We order it for you, but we sell it to whoever wants it."

"You've been ordering it for me by the case for three years. Nobody else has ever bought a bottle, except for those punks before graduation last year who took it to the new cashier, and I taught them all not to do it again. Now you're letting your average joe pick it up? What is customer service coming to? Where's the loyalty?" Gaby was ninety-nine percent sure it had been Devon, but messing with her wine was taking the secret courting thing way too far.

Megan laughed again and patted Gaby on her arm. "It went to someone who will properly appreciate it. We'll have a new case in for you next week."

"Thank you." Gaby kept her voice low as she walked

away, muttering, "Doesn't do me any good this weekend, though."

Devon had better make his move *fast*.

***

Clear nights were beautiful. It was easy to see the moon and the stars, but Devon's personal theory was that it was because all the air pollution had frozen solid and fallen back to earth. He didn't mind the cold; his body had long become accustomed to extremes in temperature.

He pulled into the parking lot of the Castor Marina and hunted for a space to park. Business was booming at the Holiday Beach Christmas Trees lot, which took over the empty space every November and December. He'd left it a little late; it was almost closing time, but the lot was still half-full with three weeks to go till Christmas. Gaby was at the trailer by the gate, paying for a little evergreen when he arrived.

"How's the tree business, Tim?" he called as he walked over from his car.

"Great. It's like money grows on them," Tim Olaffson, the tree lot manager, shot back.

Gaby didn't join in the joke. Instead, she sent Devon a death glare. "It was you!" she accused.

"Me, what?" Devon knew precisely what she was mad at. Megan had called him at the fire hall to give him a heads-up that Gaby was on the warpath over her missing bottle of Moscato. For such a bright woman, Devon could not figure out how Gaby had missed the fact that the entire town was helping him woo her.

"You are a wine thief!" she shouted.

"I didn't steal anything," he protested.

"No, you bought it, snatching it off the shelf from under my very nose."

"You said it was good."

"It was mine!"

She was a little more attached to her Moscato than he'd anticipated. "I'm sorry, Gaby, but this date is really important. She's an incredible woman, and I like her a lot."

He wanted to beat his head against the car door when she backed down at hearing him mention his mystery woman. *How could she not have a clue?*

"I'll bet she is if you are giving her my Moscato," Gaby conceded with a grunt.

"Speaking of dates," Tim started.

Oh, no! Devon shook his head furiously. Gaby wasn't ready for that.

"Speaking of dates," Tim repeated, "can I ask a favor of you, Gaby?"

"Maybe," she said cautiously.

Tim pressed ahead, his broad grin full of humor. "You know your pre-Christmas open house on Saturday night? I was talking to Lucy and Roy, and Lucy was hoping to invite a person who isn't on your list."

"It's a guy, isn't it? She wants to set me up on a blind date."

"He's a good guy. Lucy and Roy have known him for a while. He really wants to meet you."

Gaby was such a pushover for her friends. They both knew she was going to say yes before she actually said the words. "Fine. Tell Lucy's friend to bring wine. Apparently, I won't have any on hand," she added, glaring at Devon.

Once she was out of earshot, Devon leaned in. "*Lucy and Roy* have known him for a while? Way to throw your friends under the bus," he said to Tim.

"They have."

"You've *all* known me for years."

"Then I didn't lie, did I?" Tim retorted with a smirk.

Honestly, it wasn't a horrible idea. It would get him in the door with Gaby, literally. And it was the perfect place to make his move. "Okay, but if Lucy finds out what you did, it's not my fault."

CHAPTER 3

Oh, the weather outside was frightful. But fresh cookies were so delightful. And she sold mince pies to go. So let it snow, let it snow, let it snow. They were officially into the two-week countdown to Christmas, and business was booming. Gaby woke up every morning exhilarated and exhausted.

In the meantime, she had trays to fill. She could make cornbread biscuits, muffins, and flourless brownies in her sleep and nearly did. It was a balancing act to keep her regulars happy with their favorites without getting bored. She found a release for her creativity in her other recipes. Her gingerbread, rolled sugar cookies, and shortbread were popular, but they were also seasonal. People were willing to indulge in them repeatedly for a month but come January, she'd need to replace them with something else. But the new menu was a problem for another day.

After Gaby put another batch of muffins in the oven, she spent five solid minutes studying the stained recipe card in front of her. Then she glared at the ingredients on the counter. She eyed the bag of sugar and the butter especially. "Listen up. This is a Boudreau family recipe that has been handed down for four generations. I've made you before, and I'm going to make you again now. Your job is to co-operate. You are delicious, and you want all my customers to know it. Let's all work together and make some fudge!"

The butter and sugar did not respond positively to her pep talk.

It was undeniable; the fudge hated her. Forget "Merry Christmas," she was "bah, humbug" all the way. Gaby could not get the recipe to work, no matter what she tried. She couldn't understand why. She'd made it often enough with her mother when she was a kid. The super thick but unwilling-to-set chocolate sauce tasted fine, but that wasn't how it was supposed to be.

She had a moment for herself when her relief employee took over the counter at lunch. Gaby used the time to run to the post office. Peggy Zimmer behind the counter handed her a stack of envelopes. Gaby grabbed it eagerly and divided it into three piles. Junk mail—big. Bills—bigger. And fun stuff like Christmas cards—biggest. It was going to suck come January when the bills would win the contest. In the meantime, she took a minute to enjoy each card. She tucked them carefully into her purse, intending to hang them over the red and green ribbons she'd pinned to the walls behind the counter.

"Oh, fresh fudgy cookie samples!" Lucy Callahan said as Gaby hung her cards. Lucy helped herself to a handful and yipped when they burned her hand.

"They're fresh out of the oven," Gaby agreed.

"Way to warn a girl," her friend complained.

"Think of it as payback."

"For what?"

"For setting me up with a blind date in my own house."

"So, Tim talked to you about him. My friend is a good guy." Lucy ducked behind the display case and filled her travel mug with coffee. The newcomer to Holiday Beach had made herself at home in the nine months she'd been in town.

Gaby knew *Devon* was a good guy. She wanted to go out with him. If he'd ever get around to actually asking her out again. "I can attract guys just fine on my own. I don't need help," she protested.

Lucy gave her a knowing look, well aware that Gaby hadn't had a date since her last one with Devon in the spring. "Nobody's saying you do. That doesn't mean you can't take advantage of a hot guy when he falls into your lap."

A fully decked-out Jeep pulled into a parking spot in front of Butterlicious. A sandy-haired man wearing a goatee he managed to pull off hurried into the bakery, holding his fedora firmly against his head while the wind fought him for it. Josh Huntington's gray eyes were almost as pretty as Devon's brown eyes were, but Gaby noticed that Josh wasn't in his perpetual good mood.

"Good morning, Josh. What's up?" Gaby asked.

"I got some bad news," the gym owner said.

"Oh, no! Nothing too serious, I hope."

"Disappointing news is all. My brother and his family were going to come to Holiday Beach for Christmas, and they had to cancel."

"That sucks," Gaby sympathized. "Would some lemon loaf help?"

"It wouldn't hurt."

She topped up his coffee, and then Josh headed back

to his Jeep for another day of workouts and training sessions. He waved as he set his cup down on the roof, and Gaby was struck by a wave of inspiration. "Hey, Josh, wait!" She bolted outside into the cold.

"What? What's wrong?" he asked.

"I have two questions for you. First, do you want to meet me for supper on Thursday night?"

She'd never seen Josh panic before. "You and me? I thought you and Devon Sparks were…"

"That's part two. How do you feel about practical jokes?"

"I like them fine so long as they are pointed at somebody else."

Gaby grinned. "How would you like to help me pull one on Devon?"

"Devon? I owe him three or a dozen. What do you have in mind?"

Her grin grew bigger. "I'll tell you on Thursday."

Gaby's jaw dropped at the breathtakingly happy smile Josh shot her. He deserved an Oscar. She stood outside in the cold, waving as he drove away, and slowly sauntered back to Butterlicious, where her customer stared at her through the window.

"What did you do?" Lucy shouted as soon as she opened the door.

"I was my usual charming self. Now Josh and I have plans on Thursday night," Gaby replied. "For all I know, he's my blind date for Saturday anyway." Josh agreed to go along with her plan for the sole purpose of messing with Devon. All it cost her was a slight bribe of a free cookie every day until Christmas. It was a small price to pay.

"Well, he's not," Lucy protested.

"Josh is a nice guy. Cute. Likes movies. Self-employed with a booming fitness business. Technically, he's doubly employed since he is the president of the Chamber of Commerce," Gaby said, listing off her friend's qualities. "He could be the one."

"But he's not *the* guy for you."

"He's *a* guy. I invited him to the open house too, but he thinks he can only pop by for a few minutes right at the beginning, so warn your Mystery Man not to show up till later." Gaby bounced on her toes, quite pleased with herself. "Now I have two dates this week." Wait until *that* little tidbit got back to Devon. He'd learn better than to mess with her Moscato.

CHAPTER 4

He couldn't wait any longer. If he did, he risked all the good gifts vanishing like cookies left out on Christmas eve. The Starlight Gallery was doing brisk business in December. Only a couple of the larger works of art in the Holiday Beach art gallery had been sold, but several smaller items on the shelves had "Sold" signs on them. Devon wasn't worried about the blown glass figurines or the Christmas tree full of hand-stitched fabric ornaments.

He walked right through the gallery and knocked on the door leading to the stained-glass workshop at the back of the building. Samuel French was drawing on a pair of leather gloves when he noticed he had a visitor. "Good afternoon, Devon. Is it inspection time already?"

The workshop contained tanks of compressed gas, and Sam worked with an open flame. It wouldn't be the first time Devon or another member of the Bixby fire crew had popped in to verify everything was being stored and used correctly. "I'm not here in my official capacity. I'm here looking for your expert help."

"You need a Christmas present," Sam said.

"How'd you guess?"

"This is the time of year when every guy needs a Christmas present. At least you didn't opt for a poinsettia. You don't need something for your grandmother, do you?"

"No. For a girl. A woman. A special woman."

"Gabriella Boudreau," Sam said knowingly.

"Does everybody know?"

"Everybody knows that you stole her wine."

"I'll give it back!"

Sam laughed, his violet eyes crinkling at the corners. "I don't know why you keep playing games with her. One wrong move, and you're going to blow things up before you even get started."

"Can you help me out or not, Sam?" Devon asked.

"Of course. I have something I think she'll like. She was checking it out the last time she was in the shop." He pulled out a small, framed scene. A two-toned green evergreen stood in a field of snow drifts, and the image was surrounded by a red-and-white striped border that resembled a candy cane.

"It's perfect." It would fit in any window and give it a Christmassy air. But it wasn't too over the top to give as a gift to someone he liked.

Sam shrugged, then continued. "I was playing around with a design that had a glass of milk and a plate of cookies, more Santa-themed, but I haven't been able to get it right yet. Maybe next year."

That sounded like an excellent present for a baker. But Devon had no idea if he'd even make it to a second Christmas with Gaby. First, he had to figure out a way to get invited to her Christmas party to give her this gift. "I'll take this one, Sam."

They walked to the main gallery to ring up the

purchase. Mina Blackburn, the owner, was already behind the counter, her bright green manicure flashing as she wrapped tissue paper around a matched pair of ceramic candle holders and tucked them into a gift bag. "Hey, wine thief," she said in greeting.

"Not you too." Devon pointed at the frame in Sam's hands. "I'm buying Gaby a present to make up for it. I'm giving it to her at her Christmas party."

"Does she know that you're going to be her date?" Mina asked.

"She'll find out on Saturday," Devon replied with a smirk.

"You need to stop playing games, or she's going to find somebody who doesn't," Sam warned.

"I've got time." Most of the town was working with him to win Gaby over to his side and keeping her occupied until he could make his move.

Mina handed over Gaby's wrapped gift, with a bow tied around the handles in tinsel, their long ends spilling down the side of the bag. "I think what you're doing is cute, but Sam has a point. Don't wait too long. An unattached baker isn't going to stay single forever."

"Don't worry. I know what I'm doing."

***

Any distraction from the paperwork after a fire was a good one, so he happily answered his desk phone. Devon spun his chair away from the computer screen so he could look out the window. "Bixby Fire and Rescue. Devon Sparks speaking. How can I assist you?"

"Devon, what are you doing?"

He glanced down at the call display. "Lucy?"

"We've got problems."

"Do you need me to send out a truck?"

"Not fire-type problems. Gaby-type problems. She has a date on Thursday night."

He hadn't even made it home. He'd gone straight from the Starlight Gallery to the fire hall. Gaby's present was in his locker. "I didn't know she was seeing anybody. Why didn't you tell me she was seeing somebody?" This was not part of the plan. If she was involved with someone, he was going to have to bow out of the open house party. *Sam was right. I shouldn't have waited so long.*

"She's not," Lucy snitched. "I was sitting there having coffee, and Josh came in. Gaby walked him back to his car, and when she came back, she said they were going out on Thursday!"

"Diesel Fitness Josh?" This was not good. Josh Huntington was a good guy. In fact, he was known for being a good guy among the female population of Holiday Beach.

"I don't know anything about that. I do know I've been helping you for weeks to set up your big surprise on Saturday night. Fix it," Lucy ordered.

"How?" He couldn't tell his friend not to go out with a woman Devon wasn't even dating.

"I don't know. Schedule a fire drill at his gym on Thursday night or something."

That had possibilities. "I'll come up with something."

"Let me know if you need any more help," Lucy offered.

Devon ran through several ideas for how to prevent Josh from seeing Gaby on Thursday night. He worked up a sweat as he diagrammed a plan with arrows leading from one accomplice to another in an elaborate scheme until his eyes fell on the tinsel tying the gift bag handles together.

There was one fool-proof way to ensure Josh's date with Gaby never happened.

CHAPTER 5

SHE WAS GETTING CLOSER. The last batch of fudge somewhat held its shape—if she squinted at the gooey pieces the right way. When Gaby had been interrupted by a delivery, she'd pulled the pot from the element to deal with it, resulting in a batch that looked much better than it had in previous attempts. Something was niggling at the back of her brain, so she set the problem aside to let it simmer in her subconscious. If that didn't work, she'd be down to her last resort: calling her mom for help.

The lunch crowd had come and gone, cleaning out several trays in her display case. She didn't expect many more walk-ins, giving her time to get some cakes into the ovens so they'd be ready for decorating the next day.

"Gaby, are you here?"

She knew that voice. It was entirely the wrong time of day to hear it. "Devon? Is my bakery on fire?"

"Depends. Are you making fudge back there?"

She stormed to the front of her shop. "Mean!" Also wrong because she almost had the recipe right. She knew it.

Gaby stopped dead in her tracks when she saw the massive bouquet of red and white roses in his arms. That was extra mean. "For your secret girlfriend?" Gaby asked, not quite able to keep the hurt out of her voice. It wasn't right, him throwing the other woman in her face like this.

"If I'm very lucky and she says yes," Devon admitted. "So, what do you say, Gaby? Will you go out on a date with me?" He held the bouquet out to her.

She was too stunned to move. Devon's smile faltered. "Just to be clear, you were always the special person I was talking about. I'm also the blind date that Lucy and Roy arranged for your party. I was bringing your Moscato on Saturday."

Now he was asking? After all of this time? "Why?"

"I was trying to show you that I was interested by putting a lot of effort into getting a second chance with you after we fizzled this spring. But it was easier to keep dropping hints than risk you turning me down. Then someone much smarter than me told me to quit playing games because somebody might ask you out before I did, and it happened. I'm hoping I'm not too late. Even if Josh Huntington did ask you out."

"Are you jealous?"

"A little bit," Devon admitted.

"If it makes you feel any better, I'm not going to turn you down."

"That does make me feel better."

"But I can't change my plans with Josh on Thursday either. I made a commitment, and I had no reason not to do it at the time." In fact, she *couldn't* back out of her plans with Josh, and Devon was only a small part of the reason why. But Gaby didn't want to discourage him.

She'd waited too long. "I'm free for supper tonight, though."

His smile was so perfect she nearly swooned. "Me too. Can I take you out to dinner tonight, Gaby?"

"Yes. Definitely yes."

Then his cell phone rang. Devon ignored it as he threw out suggestions on where to go for supper. Their options in Holiday Beach were limited, but they could easily get into American Table on a Wednesday night. Then it rang again, this time beeping with an accompanying text. He pulled it out and groaned when he read the screen.

"What's wrong?" Gaby asked.

"There was a head-on collision south of town. One ambulance and a truck are on scene. But someone just called in a fire in Bixby, and they're short on bodies to respond," Devon said.

"You have to go," she finished

"I'm really, really sorry," Devon said. "I'll make it up to you, I swear."

"Don't worry about it. Just watch your back, okay? I've waited a while for our third date. A couple more days won't kill me." Gaby gave him a broad smile that was tainted with a drop of regret. He wanted to kiss that look right off her face.

"Rain check?" Devon asked.

"I'm working extra hours the rest of the week. Special orders for the holidays. Do I need to invite you to my open house on Saturday?"

"I think we both know I'll be there."

"It's about time." She went up on her toes and quickly pressed her lips to his cheek.

"That won't do at all." Devon glided his hands up her

arms until he had one on either side of her face. Then he bent over and kissed her for real.

"Oh, you'd better be there on Saturday. Early," Gaby whispered.

"I wouldn't miss it for the world."

CHAPTER 6

Two weeks, eight million pounds of butter and sugar, and two hundred thousand batches later, Gaby looked with glee upon the pan of fudge cooling on the baker's rack. The recipe said it would make two dozen pieces, but after so many failures, she was overcautious and had made the squares bigger than called for in case they crumbled when she cut them. It had been a needless worry. They looked perfect.

She moved twenty pieces to the serving trays, but professionalism made her sample one. For quality control. Gaby couldn't tell if the fudge was as good as she remembered or if she was so relieved that she'd finally done it that she was imagining the delicate perfection of the confection.

She wasn't going to put them out for customers. These were all for her; well, her and her party guests. Gaby was sure they would show the proper appreciation for the amount of work it had taken to make them. They'd all witnessed and offered words of encouragement during her weeks of failure. It was only right they celebrate her success with her too.

It was a shame; she could have been serving the red and white spotted fudge for weeks if she'd bothered to take the advice that her parents had been showering on her since her first freshman exam. Read the instructions. Who knew that brushing crumbs off the recipe card to get a clear look at the temperature would be so vital? Now she knew what an extra twenty degrees of heat did to fudge.

Gaby paused. Nineteen was an odd number. Eighteen meant that she could put nine on each tray if she had two, or three trays could have six each. That would be much more convenient. She picked a piece that had a little crumb broken off one corner. Eighteen worked much better.

She was slotting them into her dessert trays when she heard the crunch and squeak of the snow, indicating a vehicle had pulled into a freshly shoveled spot in front of her house. Gaby didn't have to look at the clock to know who it was.

"Hey, Devon," she called through the glass storm door since her exterior door was ajar to let guests know that they should walk right in. "Come inside." She quickly tugged at the ties of the white and green holly-print apron and hung it on the pantry door hook. She smoothed her cranberry blouse and brushed the last lingering candy cane dust from her charcoal slacks. It wasn't traditional for twenty people to tag along on a couple's date while she did all the cooking, but she and Devon had never been normal. It didn't mean she wasn't going to show him how important the evening was to her.

Heavy footfalls on the porch had her biting her lip in

anticipation, where she found evidence of her sampling. She barely wiped her mouth clean when he was there.

He wore a honey-colored cashmere sweater that brought out the light flecks in his brown eyes. She blinked when his arm came around from his back and held out the scrawniest flower she had ever seen. It looked downright pathetic compared to the huge bouquet sitting in its place of honor in the middle of her coffee table. "Thank you?" She held the thin stem carefully. "What is it?"

"Mistletoe." Devon pointed to the archway that led to her kitchen. "That looks like a good spot for it." He didn't need a chair to pin the green sprig to the top of the door frame. He looked at it from the living room, moved into the kitchen to check it from that angle, and then returned to the living room.

"What?" she asked.

He crooked his finger at her and made room for her in the narrow opening.

"What?" she repeated.

"I figured we should try this out before the others get here. I'd hate to have to tell Owen that he sold me something defective."

Gaby decided she loved firefighter logic. She loved it so much that the blood pounding in her ears during their kiss deafened her to noises outside. She jerked back in shock at the mild cough next to them.

"Hi, Gaby," Josh said. "The door was open." He didn't try to hide his smile.

Devon's chest tightened under her hands. "I thought you were kidding when you said you invited him."

"Oh, no, I was serious," Gaby said.

"Yes, Gaby and I are very serious. Our agreement stands, right?" Josh asked.

"What agreement?" Devon demanded. He thought he and Gaby had their own agreement.

"The one we made over dinner on Thursday night before our payroll program tutorial. I get two cooking lessons a month, and Gaby gets weekly yoga classes at the gym," Josh explained. A burst of laughter at the front door caught his attention. "I'll be right back. I just heard something about meatballs."

"Your date was a business meeting?" Devon asked. When the corner of Gaby's mouth turned up, he felt all the tension ease from his shoulders. "That's why you couldn't cancel. But you let me think..."

"What? Should I feel bad for letting you believe I was having dinner with Josh? You let me think you had a girl-friend for months!" His dumbstruck look was worth all the trouble it had taken to set up her "date" and the pain it had caused her when she'd had to keep a straight face. She gave him a full-throated laugh. "Come on. Admit it. You deserved it."

Devon ducked his head but laughed too. Eventually. First, he crushed her against him and whispered, "Mean," in her ear. But it was all good.

New voices streamed into the room as other Holiday Beach business owners, their dates, and assorted friends and family filled the small space. "Hi, Gabriella, merry Christmas," a teenager called from the front door.

Jordan Portman wasn't quite her niece but was rather her cousin Denny's daughter. Gaby had relocated to Holiday Beach from Louisiana a couple of years after Denny, and it had been nice to have relatives around. "Merry Christmas, Jordan."

"Do you have any of grandma's fudge?" the tall high-school senior asked.

"On the buffet." She breathed a sigh of relief that she was able to give that answer and that Jordan could report back to New Orleans that Gaby was continuing the family tradition.

"Woo-hoo, chocolate peppermint!"

"Leave some for your dad!" Gaby shouted as Jordan headed to the dining room.

Once the party was in full swing, Gaby took a moment to take everything in. All her favorite things were in one place. Good friends, good food, a safe and beautiful home. It was a good thing that Christmas was already her favorite holiday; she already had a head start on decorations. As always, her prized display was her Christmas tree. Some people liked it when nothing matched but every ornament on their tree had its own story. Gaby preferred themed trees with white lights where all the decorations were color coordinated. She'd gone with blue and white and then covered the whole thing in a thin layer of silver strands of tinsel. She thought it gave it personality, and she liked it that way.

Her festive reverie didn't last long. Devon's voice boomed across the room. "Gaby, what did you do? These fudge squares are awesome!"

*

Devon was not confessing that he was the person who had scarfed down five pieces of Gaby's fudge. She'd been right; he was glad she hadn't given up on them. It was too bad that she had hoped that some would be left over, but if the others weren't going to show the little pieces of heaven the proper appreciation, he was up for the job.

Nearly two dozen people had come and gone, but he was the only one who stuck around after Gaby finally locked the door. He helped collect plates and glasses as she flitted around, gathering remnants of the party. It was their third official date, but people treated them like they'd been together much longer. Of course, with all the visits he'd made to Butterlicious Bakery and all the time he'd spent talking to her friends about her, it felt like longer too.

Which made his present completely acceptable by Gaby's rules.

He waited till she was in the kitchen before racing to the front closet to retrieve the sparkly gold gift bag he'd hidden under his jacket.

"What is this?" Gaby asked.

"It's a Christmas present. You might have heard of the concept."

"We're exchanging presents already? I haven't..."

"I've wanted to give you a Christmas present for a long time."

She pulled out a flat, heavy square wrapped in tissue paper and looked at him suspiciously.

"Don't worry. It's not a poinsettia."

She handed him the bag, then turned the square over and over until the tissue paper fell away. She didn't say anything at all as she looked at the framed stained-glass picture. It was a beautiful winter scene. And it was the perfect size to hang in her front window so the snow-covered evergreen could be seen from the street. "It's beautiful. Thank you."

"It's not nearly as beautiful as you."

"So I got you with Josh, and you got me with the present. Are we all square now?"

"I don't think we'll ever stop having fun, but I think we can pause long enough for me to wish you a very merry Christmas," Devon said. He bent over so his lips were right in front of her. "What do you say, want to make sure that mistletoe hasn't started malfunctioning?"

"A very merry Christmas to you too, Devon," she said just before he kissed her in the glow of the Christmas tree lights.

PART THREE

THE CHRISTMAS TREE CAPER

Rookie reporter Carol French is back in Holiday Beach just in time to put her investigative skills to use. Somebody has been stealing trees from the Pine Valley Christmas Tree lot and nobody is sure if the new competition in Bixby is responsible.

Tim Olaffson is running the family Christmas tree lot on his own this year since his grandparents are vacationing in Florida. Unfortunately, someone is making off with his trees, and even spending nights on the lot isn't stopping the thefts. He has to do something before it's too late.

Carol smells a story and Tim is willing to accept help from the pretty journalist to get to the bottom of the mystery of the missing evergreens. And if they find a little romance among all the clues, it will add some much-needed cheer to his Christmas.

CHAPTER 1

Nothing warmed Tim Olaffson's heart like seeing a packed parking lot outside the Holiday Beach Christmas Trees lot. Bursts of laughter and snippets of carols rose above the general chatter of families looking for their annual evergreen. Running the lot involved a lot of long, cold hours, but for one month a year, he was happy to camp out in his trailer in the evenings and spread Christmas joy and greenery to his friends and neighbors.

Usually, he'd split the shifts with his grandparents, Bernie and Rose Olaffson, but they had announced their retirement in the fall. They were enjoying winter in Arizona and had left Tim to run the family business. They were still undecided about whether they intended to return to run the Bonfire Bay Campground the next summer as they had for decades, but Tim was happy to stick to one business a season.

Three families in a row came to pay for their trees, and after he'd helped load them and tie them down to roof racks, he noticed a familiar minivan had arrived while he was distracted. A tall man with his fluorescent orange hunting cap pointed excitedly at a nine-foot Scotch pine. As Tim expected, the young woman with almond-shaped eyes wearing a hat with two pompoms and her mother weren't far away, shaking their heads. What surprised him was the other young woman arguing boisterously with her father about the size of the tree in front of them.

"Carol! It's been forever. What are you doing back in town?" Tim asked. He hadn't seen the youngest French sibling since she'd headed off to college.

"I'm here for the annual French Christmas tree adventure," she answered. "I'm only home for the weekend right now, but I'll be back for the big day. I had to come. Mary and Mom can't handle Dad on their own. He'll come home with a tree as tall as the house if we don't rein him in."

"I'm not going to tell him his wrong," Tim said with a laugh. "Not when we sell them by the foot." He changed the subject back to her. "How long has it been since you went off to college?" He'd gone to school with Carol's big brother Sam and was still friends with him. He remembered stopping by Carol's high school graduation party and congratulating her before he and Sam took off for a guys' night out, but that had been ages ago. "Three years?"

"Five. I got my journalism degree and have been working for the *Twin City Press* for the last couple of years." She lifted her chin, probably remembering his and Sam's teasing about the gangly teenager being a hotshot reporter on the high school's online newspaper.

"Congratulations!" Five years didn't seem to have changed her much, although all he could really see were the same vivid purple eyes as her brothers and her red nose in the tiny gap between her hat brim and her scarf. "How do you like living in the city?"

"I love it. There's always something going on. Unlike…"

"Here? We're a hotbed of activity! Schultz Middle School has announced that this year's Junior Shamrock Baking Championship winner will be going to a state baking championship. Apparently, practice bakes have already begun. And rumor has it that there's going to be a new cottage development in the new year," Tim said loyally. Holiday Beach was quiet, but it wasn't dead.

"That is news. Anything felonious?"

"We had a big fire and a suspected arson last fall."

"I heard. Do you think you could rustle up something for me to report on while I'm home?" Carol asked. "I'm trying to break into the crime beat."

"Well, I've had a few trees go missing recently." Carol's eyes lit up. "But that could be lazy beavers," he said with a laugh.

"Carol, we've lost your father!" her mother called from the edge of the tree lot.

Carol grinned. "Speaking of felonies, if my dad picks out another eight-foot Scotch pine, my mother is going to murder him. I'll see you later, Tim."

"Good to see you, Carol." Mrs. French waved at him as her youngest daughter joined them before the trio disappeared into the trees.

He generally caught up with all of his neighbors when they came to the lot, but Carol had been a pleasant surprise. Sam probably would not have approved of them chatting, the overprotective big brother that he was, but Carol wasn't a teenager flirting with her big brother's best friend anymore. They were both adults now, and it was totally fine for them to catch up.

Still, Tim was grateful for the interruption. He didn't want to get into how many trees had actually gone missing from Holiday Beach Christmas Trees this season. He'd only been open for ten days, and he'd already lost more than he had in the last two years combined. His grandfather had placed the orders the previous year, so Tim couldn't control how many trees they were getting, but he was certain he was going to run out of evergreens before he ran out of customers. He was planning a trip out to Norman Tree Farm to see if they could provide him with any extra stock.

More families came to the trailer to pay for their trees. Tim spent ten minutes trying to balance a massive white spruce on the roof of the Trans' dark blue SUV. Then he clanged the brass handbell they used to signal to folks that the lot was closing in fifteen minutes, encouraging them to make their final selections.

Finally, he was down to the last two families. "Carol, did the three of you keep your father in check?" he asked.

"Barely. Mary and Mom are waiting in the car while I make sure Dad doesn't try to make a last-minute swap," she joked.

"I'm right here, you know," Mr. French grumbled.

"We love you, Dad. We just can't leave you unsupervised. I promised Mary."

Mr. French looked at Tim for support. "I live with three grinches. Tell me, Tim, where are all the big trees this year?"

He shrugged. "This is what we got from the Norman Tree Farm. I'm going to take a trip out there tomorrow to see if I can pick up any extra trees they have. Should I look for a bigger one for you?"

"No!" Carol shouted.

Mr. French sighed dramatically. "I seem to have been overruled."

"I'll talk Mom into letting you use tinsel this year to make up for it, no matter how much the cat hates it," Carol promised.

This was one of the things Tim loved about working on the lot. He was never bored. "I'll let you know anyway, Mr. French."

"You're a good boy, Tim."

While Mr. French went to his car to get some bungee cords, Carol sidled closer to the payment desk. "So, Tim, do you want company on your trip to the tree farm?" she asked.

"You? Why?"

"It would be a good human-interest piece. I could also pitch it to the green section too. Live Christmas trees are making an environmental comeback. I'll split the gas with you."

For a second, Tim thought Carol was flirting with him. But if this was just a business trip, he'd rather have the company. "Sure, if you'd like."

"I'd like. Give me your phone," she ordered. She grabbed it after he called up his contact list, took a selfie, and entered her name and number. "Give me at least half an hour's notice tomorrow, and I'll be ready to go. I can meet you here."

"I can pick you up," Tim said. "I'm pretty sure I can still find your house since I practically lived there in high school."

She smiled at him, then winked. "I'll be waiting."

CHAPTER 2

"I'M GOING to help Dad get the tree in the stand and water it, but I promise we won't put a single ornament on without you." Carol hugged her sister goodnight and returned to the living room.

Her father was glaring at the tree lying in the middle of the floor. "Do you want to hold the tree or be underneath it and screw it in place?"

"I've got better knees. I'll fight with the stand," she said. Carol was used to it; her father's knees had been bad for years. Sam would offer to do it if he was home, but he was working extra hours at this stained-glass studio this month, trying to keep up with the demand for his colorful art. The outing to choose the Christmas tree was all the disruption her parents were willing to cause Mary for one night, although her sister was capable of holding the tree if her dad manipulated the stand. This way, the tree would be up, and tomorrow evening would be set aside as family time for decorating it. Sam had already promised to make an appearance.

As she got into position, her dad hit her with a question she couldn't avoid. "So, do you still have a crush on that Tim fellow?"

Laying on the floor, hands covered in sap, with evergreen needles stuck in her hair, Carol groaned. "No, Dad. I haven't been harboring a secret Tim obsession for the last five years. I'm not in high school anymore. And he isn't either." Yes, she'd mooned over her big brother's best friend in school. And maybe she did ask about him, a lot, when she came home during her first year at college, but that was in the past. She wasn't a hormonal teen anymore. She had a job and a life waiting for her. Any flirting she was considering now that she was back for the holidays was strictly recreational.

Thankfully, Tim had the good sense to text her the next day at a very reasonable nine o'clock in the morning. Carol dressed in layers and was waiting at the front window for Tim's pickup to pull to the curb. She had her phone, her old digital camera tucked in her inside jacket pocket, and an old-fashioned notebook and mechanical pencil in case her phone's battery died from the cold. More importantly, she was wearing the lilac scarf Mary knit for her. It brought out her eyes, and she added a fresh application of Holiday Hollyberry red lipstick to make a good impression... for the tree lot owner that she wanted to interview. She wanted to look professional and not like some Christmas tree customer off the street. The fact that Tim would also get the benefit was completely coincidental.

"How are your grandparents doing?" she asked as she settled in for the drive.

"Good. Every time I send them a text telling them how the lot is doing, they respond with a photo of a palm tree."

"I love them!"

Tim smiled. "I do too. They deserve this. I'm starting to doubt that they'll be coming back for any reason other than to vacation for the summer. I don't think they're going to want to go back to running the campground."

"How about you? Would you do it?" The Bonfire Bay Campground was a local institution. It was packed from Veteran's Day weekend to Labor Day with weekend tourists along with some heartier souls who camped in the off-season.

"I'm not going anywhere. I'll be happy to take it over full-time. It makes for a long, busy summer, but I get to be outside all day, every day." His face confirmed the truth of his words. Even in December, he still had a lingering tan.

"That's from May till October. And the Christmas tree lot is November and December. What are you going to do this spring?" Carol asked.

"Probably show up at my grandparents' door in Phoenix and tell them they have a roommate for a couple of weeks," Tim said with a laugh. "I'll need that long to defrost."

"A hot vacation sounds wonderful." Carol had gone to Mexico two years ago on a whirlwind five-day vacation package. The memories of sunshine, beaches, and good friends inspired her to start saving for another trip as soon as she got home. Unfortunately, it was still at least another winter away.

"I'll send you a picture of a palm tree," he teased.

Tim's truck cruised down the highway on the sunny day, unrolling a scenic vista of snow-covered evergreens and bare branches against a cold, clear blue sky. Traffic was sparse, mostly commercial trucks and the occasional personal vehicle. "We're almost there. Nathanial Norman owns the Norman Tree Farm. They've supplied us for years, but I think Mr. Norman is about the same age as my grandparents. I wouldn't be surprised to hear if he's looking at retirement too."

Tim pulled off the highway up a plowed but snow-packed gravel road. It ended half a mile away at an open gate. A dirty patch of clear land was home to a small fishing shack with a chimney and a few parked vehicles. A large rental truck with an out-of-season summer lake scene painted on the side was parked at the end of the clearing, its back doors open wide. Two men in plaid flannel jackets exited the shack when Tim beeped his horn in greeting.

"Mr. Olaffson," the bigger, bearded one called.

"Hello, Mr. Norman."

"How are your grandparents? How's the lot?"

"They're currently sunning themselves, probably on a pickleball court, in Arizona, laughing at their poor grandson being knee-deep in Minnesota snow. Which is great for them. As for the lot, it's surprisingly empty already. A few—well, more than a few of our trees have grown legs and walked away all by themselves. I'm hoping you might have some extra stock. I'm willing to help cut them down if I have to."

"That's not necessary. My new partner is working with me this year, learning the business. But you know that since he's been making your deliveries. Elton, come over and say hello."

Carol was surprised to see Mr. Norman's partner was her age, but nobody she recognized as local. He was taller and darker than Tim but clean-shaven, unlike his boss. He was also more willing to flirt by the big smile she got. "I'm Elton Wise. How can we help you today?"

"Carol French, *Twin Cities Press*. Unofficially. I'm tagging along with Tim hoping to get some background for a green Christmas piece about the resurging popularity of live trees."

"I'd love to give you a tour." At his boss's cough, Elton added, "After we take care of Mr. Olaffson's business, of course. What do you need, sir?"

"Three dozen more trees, at least. I'll take any variety, any size."

Mr. Norman looked at Elton, who shook his head. "I'm sorry," Elton said. "We picked up a couple of new contracts this year, and we ended up selling every last tree. We didn't hold anything back." He held up his hands. "Mr. Norman had been seeing fewer sales for the last couple of years, so he brought me on to increase the business."

Mr. Norman agreed. "Miss French, you are right about this being a growing industry. I wasn't taking proper advantage of it. Young Elton proposed a new business plan, and I must say that he's delivered. I'm sorry that we can't help you, Tim."

Elton gave Tim an appraising look. "I supposed we could take a look through next year's growth. We might be able to squeeze out a dozen trees for a long-time customer like the Holiday Beach Christmas Trees lot. I came up with the business plan, but Mr. Norman has the experience. He's been teaching me about customer loyalty."

The older man slapped Elton on the back. "And I'm thrilled that you're picking it up. I was just about to suggest that. How do you feel about a dozen trees, Tim?"

"I'll take what I can get and be grateful for them," Tim said. But based on their conversation in the car, Carol knew he was disappointed. Tim was deeply concerned about the lot's ability to provide for all its customers.

"Why don't you two have a look at that field, and this young lady and I will talk turkey about the Christmas tree business?" Mr. Norman suggested. "Come into the warming hut with me, Miss French, and I'll answer all your questions."

Tim looked relieved at the suggestion. "Go ahead. I won't leave without you."

Carol expected a blast of hot air filled with the funk of sweaty bodies and no ventilation. Instead, there was a small wood stove, a pair of hardbacked wooden chairs, and a cooler acting as a table. The room was heavily scented with pine. "Please, call me Carol," she asked.

"Let me guess, Carol," Mr. Norman said to her. "Folks have rediscovered the glaring discrepancy between the carbon footprint numbers when it comes to shipping an artificial tree across the Pacific from China versus the sustainable cost of processing locally grown evergreens that have the benefit of being fully compostable."

Carol grinned as she pulled out her phone and turned on the recording app. "Yes, that's exactly it, Mr. Norman. Let's chat."

CHAPTER 3

THE NEW GUY wasn't so bad when he wasn't flirting with Carol, Tim could admit to himself. That didn't mean he was going to give Elton the opportunity to talk to her. She could get all the information she needed from Mr. Norman.

"It's great that you're doing so well. I remember Mr. Norman not even clearing his entire sections in the past few years," Tim said.

"That new lot in Bixby is helping a lot. They're getting all their white spruce from us, but they have another source for their Fraser and balsam firs."

Tim nodded in understanding. He spread out his suppliers too. "I appreciate you dipping into next year's trees for us. Will you be increasing the number of seedlings you plant from now on?" It took about a decade to grow a good-sized, six-foot Christmas tree, so any changes they made now wouldn't be profitable for years.

"Yes, I've already made the calls to various nurseries. We're going to be busy planting this spring. With

Nathaniel looking to sell the business, anything we do now will increase what he can get for it," Elton said.

"I figured he'd be selling soon." Trips to the Norman Tree Farm had been part of Tim's life long before he started working on the lot. When he was a kid, he'd come out with his grandparents and "pick" the tree for his family, calling dibs in months before any of the trees made it to market. It was bittersweet to hear he wouldn't be dealing with the same man anymore. "He deserves the break."

"I'm sure the next owners will be happy to keep working with you. Maybe it'll be somebody local. Holiday Beach seems like a nice area with friendly people. Like your sister, Carol."

The guy was definitely fishing for information on Carol. "Not my sister. Family friend. Very close, long-time family friend. We have a ... special relationship." "Special" in that he used to ruffle her hair when she was Sam's irritating little sister. But Elton could interpret his comment any way he wanted.

Their arrival at the treeline cut their conversation short. They quickly found a dozen trees that had outgrown the rest. Elton cut down a thirteenth as well, saying it was for luck. The two men dragged the trees to the end of the row. "I'll wrap these and drop them off in Holiday Beach by the end of the day tomorrow if that works for you."

Tim nodded. "That would be great timing. I'll still be getting my regular restock next week too?"

"You're already in the books. You'll get a full ship-ment," Elton confirmed.

They shook hands, agreement made, and tromped

across the snow-covered field back to Tim's truck. They heard Carol and Mr. Norman laughing before they opened the shack door. "Are you done already?" Carol asked.

"Yep, all finished."

She stood, brushing cookie crumbs off her lap. "Thanks for the talk, Mr. Norman. I'll let you know if the paper decides to run the story."

"It was a pleasure to meet you, Carol."

They were halfway back to town when Carol spoke again. "Don't forget that I owe you a coffee for taking me along, Tim."

"You don't have to."

"A promise is a promise. Would you prefer By the Cup or American Table? My mom says that American Table has a Christmas cookie dessert tray right now." She raised her eyebrows at him. "She says they have ginger-bread cookies."

"My weakness." At first, he was surprised she remembered that odd fact about him. Not many people would remember their brother's best friend's Christmas cookie preferences. Tim knew that Carol preferred whipped shortbread, but that was only because she had issued threats annually if anybody dared to eat any. But that wasn't strange. He also knew that the middle French sibling's favorite was peanut butter balls. Mary's love for peanut butter eclipsed all other food and was unlikely to ever change.

"You know I won't turn down gingerbread. American Table it is." It wasn't a date, it was a business transaction, so Tim had to treat it like one. "Was Mr. Norman helpful?"

"The man's been in the tree business for decades, so he was the perfect interview. Besides, everybody loves the old curmudgeon who is actually a Santa at heart."

"That's only half of your article, right? For the other half, you need to interview somebody who sells Christmas trees to get the whole picture of the industry."

"You're right," Carol agreed.

Just when he was about to ask her what she wanted to ask him, she continued. "I guess I could talk to the folks who own that new Christmas tree lot in Bixby. Elton says they're very friendly."

"You know what, Carol? You're still a brat."

She laughed loudly, drawing the hostess's attention as they walked into one of Holiday Beach's favorite restaurants. "Of course, I want to talk to you, Tim. What good is a newbie to the business when I have an experienced old-timer who can tell me what's changed over the years?"

"Now I'm old?"

"Neither of us are kids anymore," Carol said.

"No, we're not. But we're not old, either."

"I'm glad you agree." She smiled at him like he'd said something profound, but Tim had no idea what it was. If Carol was happy with him for any reason, he'd take it.

She ordered herself a hot cocoa and a cookie plate, and he did the same. He expected her to launch into questions about work, but she asked about his other job instead, enquiring about how the campground was doing.

Carol had been home twice over the summer, but he had been working and missed her. They had crossed paths briefly the previous Christmas. It had been long enough for him to see her but not long enough for him to notice that she'd grown up while she'd been away.

"You covered the big tornado last October?" he asked in amazement.

Carol shrugged. "It was more luck than skill at first. I was in the area doing background research for one of the paper's reporters, so I was there when it hit, and I got some decent footage. Since it took out my rental car, the paper had me cover the aftermath too."

"That sounds terrifying." He wouldn't have wanted to be there, let alone be out getting videos of the storm. But for Carol, it was part of her job, and it had to be done. Whether she was scared or not.

"No, terrifying is taking over and running a family business. I'd be petrified of messing up. Aren't you under a ton of pressure from your parents and grandparents?"

"Not really. Obviously, I want to do well for them, but they've been teaching me the ropes for years. And I can always call them if I have a question."

Carol nodded reluctantly. "Let's leave it at we have different ideas of stressful jobs."

"Look at us with our grown-up jobs. We can talk about mortgages and those pesky kids next door playing on the lawn next."

"As we have our very child-like hot chocolate and Christmas cookies?"

"We're adults; we're not dead."

Carol laughed with him. "If the campground is going well, how's the Christmas tree business? What were you saying about stolen trees?"

"Every year, we expect a few trees to go missing. A couple desperate families. A few jerks. Miscounting deliveries. But this year..." A big breath exploded from his lungs. "I have no idea what's going on this year. Elton dropped off a load. I signed for it and unloaded it into the holding area. I showed up the next morning, and two dozen were missing. That would fill the back of a pickup truck. Nobody saw anything. And that was just the first time. I've been hit again since then. I know that fifty trees don't sound like a lot..."

"Yes, it does. That could be ten percent of your yearly income."

His jaw dropped when she spouted off that number. "Mr. Norman taught you well. So you can see why I'm concerned and why I'm glad to even get another dozen trees from Norman Tree Farm. We can't afford to lose any more."

"Do you know if it's just your lot? Do you want to go down to that new place in Bixby with me? We can ask if they've had any problems. It could be another angle for my story."

On the one hand, it was a good excuse to spend more time with Carol. On the same hand, it was an opportunity to check out the competition. "Sure. When? Tonight?"

"I can't. Family night. We're decorating the tree this evening and having snacks while we do it. Mary has been talking about it for weeks."

"Tomorrow?"

"We'd have to do it early. Or take separate cars. I'm heading back into Minneapolis for work on Monday."

"Tomorrow works. Maybe you'll have enough information to write your article by then." And that meant he'd have an excuse to get her number. Of course, he'd want to follow up on a news story he was in.

Their cookies didn't last long. But their post-trip snack ended before Tim was ready. Sam's little sister was all grown up now, and he was glad he was going to spend more time with her. "Noon tomorrow?" he said. "I'll be able to get back to the lot to open at two o'clock."

"And I can drive back to the city in daylight. Sounds like a plan."

CHAPTER 4

CAROL and her brother were sitting on the sofa, a box of pepperoni pizza on the coffee table in front of them. They each took another slice as they waited for the middle French sibling to find the perfect spot for her last ornament.

"How's Mary doing?" Carol asked quietly. Although she got regular updates from her parents, she wanted to hear what Sam had to say.

Her brother took a bite before answering, hissing when the hot cheese hit the roof of his mouth. "Holding steady. She's still working part-time, washing dishes four days a week at Colombo's. She and Dad renewed their positions as volunteer representatives with the local Down's Syndrome organization. But she caught a cold in the fall that she hasn't managed to shake yet."

Mary shook her head when her mom pointed at an empty branch. "She seems happy," Carol said.

"She's always happy. She was very excited that you were coming home this weekend. I'm glad you didn't ask if you could leave early tonight to hang out with a certain Christmas tree salesman."

"You aren't going to give me a hard time about Tim, are you?"

"No. You're a grown woman, and you can see who you want." Then Sam waggled a scarred, calloused finger in her face. "I'm going to warn Tim that if he does anything that he even thinks might upset me, I'm going to ban his trees from the Starlight Gallery and tell Mina to refuse to lend him any decorations for his model trees at the lot."

"You wouldn't!"

"I would."

Her brother's stained-glass ornaments were hugely popular. He made them year-round to create a stockpile for the holiday season when they sold out so quickly. In December, they were the main attraction in the Starlight Gallery, where he had a studio in the back. Every year, the owner Mina put a huge tree in the middle of the main space, lit it with hundreds of tiny white lights, and let Sam's genius speak for itself. It wouldn't be the same if they didn't use a Holiday Beach Christmas tree. "Mina would never let you. Besides, shouldn't you be more concerned if he does something to upset me rather than upset you?"

"I don't think you'd be upset if he kissed you."

"Tim hasn't kissed me!"

"But he may want to."

And Carol would let him. But she wasn't about to get into a fight with her brother in the family living room about it.

"Okay, I'm done," Mary told them, beaming. She pointed at her glitter-covered gingerbread man hiding behind a veil of silver tinsel. The Frenches always had a red-and-white-themed tree. The only exceptions were the ornaments they'd created over the years. Sam had added some stain-glassed ones. Mary's were hand-painted plaster-of-Paris. Carol had cross-stitched a pair for each family member when she was a teenager, although she hadn't picked up a needle since she'd graduated from high school.

"It looks great, Mary. Are we done now?"

"Mom and Dad still need to put the star on top."

The three siblings sat on the sofa, posing as their mother took a photo. Carol didn't get home as often as she'd like, and she missed her family when she was in the city. She wasn't drowning in homesickness, though. Living in downtown Minneapolis had its perks. She had a good job and a nice apartment, and lots of friends. It wasn't quite perfect, but she was happy enough for now and enjoying each day as it came.

The next morning, with her trunk acting as a freezer for a bag full of leftovers, and after hugging her family, Carol followed Tim's truck south. Half an hour later, they pulled into the parking lot of E.L.F. Evergreen Emporium.

"Elf?" Carol asked when Tim opened her car door.

"Emma and Lance Ferguson. Husband-and-wife team. It looks like they're doing good business." A temporary chain link fence formed a square around four distinct areas. In each of three corners was a different species of Christmas tree, while the fourth was reserved for a little heated trailer and a sitting area for families. The sign in front said they were open from noon till eight in the evening. Luckily there were only a couple of families wandering around. A woman in a blue ski jacket and Santa hat waved as they entered.

"Tim, is that you?"

"Hi, Emma. This is Carol French. We're checking out the competition today. How's your first year going?"

"We severely underestimated how many space heaters we needed in our little trailer. Other than that, it's not bad," the other woman said with a laugh. "Hi, Carol. I'm Emma Ferguson. My husband Lance is around here somewhere. Are you working with Tim in Holiday Beach?"

"Not exactly. I'm researching a possible story for my paper about the rise in popularity of live Christmas trees. I've spoken to Tim, and to Nathaniel Norman at Norman Tree Farm, but I'd love to get the opinion of somebody new to the business. Tim says this is your first year?" Carol asked. Then she had to pay attention to the answer. This whole article had only been an excuse to spend more time with Tim, but now she was getting invested in the idea.

Emma happily offered her a quick tour and answered all of her questions. Carol was forced to leave Tim behind, but she regrouped with him about ten minutes later, finding him chatting with Emma's husband. "These folks got lucky. Elton Wise was able to give them a full restock," Tim told her.

Lucky? That sounded questionable to her reporter's ears. The thought that Elton had a new deal with an up-and-coming business in a larger town and intended to undercut a long-standing client to drive the smaller lot under was suspicious. But then the innocent-looking pair added a couple of details that blew Carol's conspiracy theory apart.

"Half a restock," Lance corrected. "But it was enough to help. We had a break-in last week. They stole four dozen trees. If a neighbor hadn't been out walking their dog, it would have been a lot more. Now one of us is on the lot every night."

"I'm glad it's only going to be for another three weeks," Emma added. "It's a shame it's necessary. They're Christmas trees, for goodness's sake. But we have to. Lance heard a truck pull up a couple of nights ago."

"The same night I got hit," Tim said.

"Fortunately, the light scared them off," Emma continued. "But now we know we can't afford to take any chances. We've always got somebody on guard now."

"I'm going to have to start doing that," Tim said. "I can't afford to lose any more."

This was a twist to the story Carol hadn't anticipated. Before she could dig deeper, a convoy of cars pulled into the parking lot.

"You've got customers arriving, and I need to get back to my own lot. Thanks for your time," Tim said.

"Yes, thanks for talking to me," Carol echoed.

She stomped her feet to keep the blood flowing as she and Tim stood awkwardly between their vehicles in the parking lot. "That many trees going missing on that many lots isn't desperate families or jerks. That's planned," she told him.

"An organized Christmas-tree-stealing ring?"

"They probably exist somewhere. Why not in Minnesota?" If there was one thing that she'd learned from working at the paper, it was that people were capable of *anything*. Stealing trees at Christmas wasn't a stretch at all. "What are you going to do?"

"Start standing watch, I guess. If this is deliberate, I can't afford not to."

"What about getting a security system? Your place is only a couple of minutes away. If you get a motion sensor alarm, you could be there before they're done and catch them in the act." The thought of Tim sleeping in that little camper on the lot, night after night, made her heart hurt. She knew that he had two part-time employees, but she also knew he'd never ask them to take a guard shift unless he was too sick or rundown to do it himself.

He slapped his leather mittens together as he contemplated her idea. "Motion sensor alarm. And lights. It might be worth the investment since I'd be able to use them again," he said thoughtfully.

A cold wind gusted through the lot, stirring up snowflakes. As much as she wanted to have a few more minutes with Tim, she wasn't about to risk frostbite for it. "Text me about what you decide to do."

"And you text me about the story if the paper decides to run it," he replied. Tim looked like he wanted to ask her something, but he ducked his chin into his scarf instead. "Have a good drive back to the city."

"Thanks. I'll see you next time I'm in town," Carol said. She drove away, leaving Tim waving in the rearview mirror.

CHAPTER 5

One week later

With two weekends to go before Christmas, Tim was ready to lock the gates on Holiday Beach Christmas Trees for the evening and give himself the rest of the night off. Even with two part-time assistants, he was still on the lot seven days a week, even the Tuesdays when they were closed. And he'd slept on site for five of those nights. On the second, he thought he heard a truck pull up, but by the time he'd turned on the exterior lights and gotten dressed, he hadn't seen a thing.

On the sixth day, the security system he'd ordered from Handler Hardware arrived. Julie Handler had brought it over herself and had helped him install it. Now he had motion-sensor lights around the perimeter fencing and a motion-activated camera directed at the gate. Thanks to the Wi-Fi at the gas station next door, the camera was attached to a computer that sent an alarm to his phone when it was triggered.

The first night he'd spent in his own bed in a week had been the best sleep of his life.

Equally important, he hadn't lost a single tree all week. Elton had been as good as his word and had dropped off the thirteen trees he and Tim had picked out, plus an additional five smaller ones. Tim took them, not complaining about paying full price for them. Then he'd received his regularly scheduled resupply. As long as no more were stolen, he'd still end the year with a decent profit.

With a secure business in his back pocket and a night off since a cold, blowy front had scared away most of his customers, Tim decided he had a couple of hours to be social. He hadn't seen most of his friends since Thanksgiving, so after a couple of texts, they had plans to meet.

Sam hadn't warned him that he was bringing his baby sister along to the Escape Room.

Carol waved when he arrived, and by the time he'd ordered his first drink, she'd claimed a stool at his small round table. "You didn't text me this morning."

"I didn't have anything to report. I installed the camera and lights yesterday. Nothing happened overnight. Which is good, right?"

"Yes, it's good, but you still should have texted. Even one of your terrible jokes."

"I'm sorry. Not about the jokes, though."

Carol had texted him excitedly on Monday to tell him a story mentioning him was going to appear in the paper later that week. He reported that he'd ordered a security system. She let him know that Colombo's Restaurant, where her sister worked, had added a gingerbread cake to the menu. He had no news to offer, but he didn't want her to stop texting, so he sent her a Christmas tree joke. Then another, and another.

She didn't tell him to stop, and her responses with various movie characters face-palming led into a conversation about movies, which lead to more late-night conversations while he was alone in the trailer.

It had been the best part of his week.

"I'll be back in a minute, and then we can discuss the next step in our investigation," she said.

"We aren't conducting an investigation," Tim yelled at her back as she ran over to give an old school friend a hug. He took the interruption as an opportunity to text her another joke. Carol glanced at her phone, typed something quickly, and kept talking to her friend.

Tim grinned at her one-word response.

Better.

If Carol wanted a daily text, she'd get one. When he ran out of tree puns, he had enough reindeer jokes to get him through the rest of the holidays.

When she returned, she immediately returned to her investigation idea. "You and I will continue to stake out the tree lot. We have Sheriff Gillespie programmed on speed dial. When the thieves pull up, you hit the lights. Then while they're distracted, I run around the back and move my car to block the entrance to the street. We'll catch them red-handed," she proposed. Her blond ponytail bobbed up and down as she nodded, encouraging him to agree with her.

"How about no? A big bucket of nope. Except for having the sheriff on speed dial. That's fine. But you and I aren't going to spend the night in that icebox when I have a perfectly good alarm system," Tim protested. The company would be delightful, right up to the point when

Carol realized she was getting frostbite. Taking her to the emergency room would probably adversely affect his chances for a date after that. "See, everything is fine."

He called up the camera's live feed and turned the screen to face her.

"A person of suspicious bearing is loitering outside the gate," she told him.

"Ha ha, very funny."

Carol grabbed his hand and turned the phone, so he could see it. The alarm on his phone went off at the same time. "A person of suspicious bearing is loitering outside my gate!" He couldn't see the person's face, but it was a tall man, going by the stature and gait. Tim couldn't see a vehicle because the camera was positioned to only pick up activity at the entrance, but the person was backlit by headlights. The figure moved closer, activating the motion-sensitive lights.

"We can be there in five minutes," Carol said quietly. "You drive. I'll call the sheriff on the way."

He nodded once and grabbed his jacket. Carol followed him out the door.

She was dead on in her estimate. She was just ending her call with the Holiday Beach Police Department when the lot came into sight. The front gate was open, and the security lights were blazing, but they couldn't see any sign of an intruder. No people. No cars. Nothing but an empty lot with a spooky atmosphere that felt more like Halloween than Christmas.

"Where'd they go?" she asked.

Tim shrugged. "Maybe the lights scared them off."

"They still managed to open the gate."

He put his hand on the door handle, but Carol jerked his arm back. "Wait for the sheriff."

"I want to see if they cut the lock." The first time he'd been robbed, he assumed the lock hadn't closed properly. The second time, the destroyed lock looked like it had been bashed with a brick. If they were getting bolder and more experienced, he expected them to be prepared with a bolt cutter this time.

"I didn't see any trucks go by. Did you?" she asked.

It was a good question. The thieves had to be using a half-ton pickup at the very least to carry the number of trees that went missing. A large cargo van might be enough, but it would be a tight squeeze for a driver and a dozen six-to-eight-foot evergreens. He and Carol had driven from the Escape Room, followed the highway into town where it became Lakeside Drive, and come out on the other side at the marina at the town limits, where their road turned into the highway again. It had been quiet at that hour, with only a handful of cars and minivans on the streets. But he didn't remember seeing any trucks. "No, I didn't."

Carol stayed in his truck when the sheriff's SUV pulled up. Aaron Gillespie unfolded his lanky frame from the driver's seat and waved Tim over. The two of them walked through the rows of trees and all around the inside of the fence, checking to see if any other areas had been cut open. They hadn't.

"I take it this security system is new?" Aaron asked him as he stood in the trailer door while Tim pulled a new lock out of a cupboard drawer.

"I put it in two days ago."

"Good investment."

"I'll say. Do you think they'll be back, or should I spend another night in here on guard?" Tim asked.

The sheriff shook his head. "They won't be back

tonight if they come back at all. They weren't expecting anybody to know they were here. The lights probably lit up the camera, and the last thing they want is to be noticed. Spend the night in your own bed. I'll have my deputies do more frequent drive-bys of this area and light it up when they pass by. How many more days are you open?"

"How many more days till Christmas?" He did a quick calculation in his head. "Fourteen."

"Did you see anything? Any identifying marks? Any vehicles?"

"Nothing like that. The vehicle was out of sight. All we saw was a man in a dark ski jacket and jeans."

"Oh, that guy. He'll be easy to find," the sheriff joked. "Stop by the station tomorrow to fill out a proper report. In the meantime, I suggest taking your date someplace where she can warm up." Aaron waved at Carol, who waved back through the windshield. "I know Sam's headed to the Escape Room, so you might want to consider a glass of wine at Colombo's before they close in an hour."

When they arrived at Colombo's fifteen minutes later, Carol didn't want wine. She did order a cup of minestrone, which sounded like a really good idea, so he had one as well.

"We're going to get this guy," Carol said with conviction.

"We can't be sure of that."

"We can if we help Sherriff Gillespie."

"I'm not sure he'll appreciate that," Tim said. Aaron Gillespie might only be the sheriff of a small area around Holiday Beach, but the man got the job done. He didn't need amateur help from them. Although Tim wasn't at all surprised that Carol wanted to dive into the now-official case. She was definitely a "get involved" person. In everything.

"I'm not talking about staking out the tree lot. Again," she said pointedly. "But we have the facts. There was somebody there tonight. They would have needed a large vehicle to transport the number of trees that had been stolen. And since they aren't Santa Claus, it wouldn't have been a sleigh, which means they would have needed to drive—"

"Down Lakefront Drive," Tim said slowly, coming to the same realization that Carol had already reached.

"Since the highway turns into Lakefront Drive, there is a ninety-nine-percent chance they had to drive down it. It's possible that they drove in from somewhere north and went back the same way, but I can't see a big need for black-market Christmas trees that way," she said. "I've been doing my research. There are a lot of family farms and lots up there that serve the communities. The big demand is south."

Tim nodded. "That makes sense. But how does knowing the escape vehicle would have driven down Lakeside Drive help us?"

Carol shook her complimentary breadstick at him. "You'll never be a detective, Tim. Who would have seen a truck driving down the street?"

"At that hour? Nobody. Everything was closed."

"Security cameras never close, Tim.

He wanted to smack his own forehead. He didn't know if By The Cup had a surveillance camera, but he could think of at least two businesses along that strip that did. "What are we looking for?"

"Any trucks or cargo vans that went by within, what, ten minutes of your alarm going off?" she proposed.

He should have figured that out on his own. "Ten minutes should do it. Fifteen on the outside in case they staked out the lot for a few minutes to make sure everybody was gone." He couldn't believe it. They had an actual lead.

Tim's spoon scraped the bottom of his bowl. "We can't do any more tonight. Do you want to make the rounds with me tomorrow to the various businesses? Be my partner in crime prevention?" Two people could get the job done in half the time. And she was much prettier than Sheriff Gillespie.

"I'd love to, partner."

CHAPTER 6

It was her last day in Holiday Beach before she came back for the holiday weekend. Carol had pushed through her usual procrastination and had brought home her family's gifts two weeks early, setting them under the tree to tease and tempt her family while she wasn't there. That way, when she came home on Christmas Eve, all she needed to bring would be a suitcase full of clothes and all the last-minute groceries her mother requested from the specialty grocery stores in Minneapolis.

She hadn't planned on spending her final morning visiting every single business in town. It didn't matter how many layers she wore or how many times she wound her scarf around her neck—after the third time she stepped into the cold wind coming off the lake, she began questioning her desire to move over to the crime beat.

It took them six visits to hit paydirt. Riesling and Brie, a wine and cheese store that catered to tourists in the summer and locals all year long, had a sophisticated security system that happened to include a camera on the front door that caught all of the street traffic.

Megan Mulroney was happy to show them the footage from the previous night. "What are we looking for?" the tanned woman asked as she called up the file on her office laptop.

"Street view. About nine o'clock last night. We can eliminate any cars or SUVs," Carol told her.

Tim didn't hover over the screen as she did. Maybe because he was taller than she was, and he could see over her shoulder. Or maybe he didn't have any faith in her idea and thought she was just wasting their time.

But he got very close when Megan paused the playback when a five-ton rental truck entered the frame. "Something like that?" she asked.

"Exactly like that," Tim said.

Unfortunately, there was no way for them to identify the truck aside from the rental company name and its lakeside logo printed on the side. They didn't have a shot of the license plate or a good view of the driver. "So, this was a bust after all," Carol said with a sigh.

"Maybe Sheriff Gillespie can work some magic," Megan said. "I'll call him to come pick up a copy of the footage."

"Thanks, Megan."

Since By the Cup was half a block away, Carol pulled Tim into the coffee shop to regroup. "Well, we confirmed one thing. It wasn't some random guy. It was a plan for a big haul."

"You're right. We stopped them last night, but I can't guarantee I'll get that lucky again," Tim said. "We responded very quickly yesterday. If they try again when I'm at home asleep, it'll take me longer. By the time I make it to the lot, they could clean me out." He sighed. "I am not looking forward to sleeping in the trailer for the next two weeks."

When Rachel Best, the coffee shop owner, brought over their coffees, he rallied. "Thanks, Rachel, Tim said. "And thanks, Carol. At least we know what we know now. Folks can be on the lookout I'll call Emma at E.L.F. and let her know what we've discovered. It's a start."

Even with the coffee boost, he locked tired. Much more tired than he had a week earlier. The poor guy was barely into his thirties. He shouldn't be moving like he was fifty. "I do have one more idea," Carol said hesitantly. "But you've already spent so much on the security system."

"I invested in a security system, and it has already paid off. What are you thinking?" Tim asked.

Carol took a breath because this idea was *way* out there. "Have you heard of Never-Lost Luggage Chips?"

"Not really."

"It's like a luggage tag, only it has a little GPS tracker in it. If your luggage goes missing, you can track it with an app as long as there's accessible Wi-Fi," she explained. She had a flight attendant friend who swore by it.

"You want me to put a GPS chip in my Christmas trees?"

"Not all of them. Just a couple. Put the tracker in at night and take them out when you reopen the next day to recharge them."

Tim didn't look convinced. "That's not going to stop the thefts."

"No, but it will allow you to track down trees if they go missing," she said. It was a long shot and might not even be necessary, but she was invested now. She needed to know who was stealing the trees and where they were going. Carol wondered if the motive was money or something more, but she could discover that after they busted the tree-thieving syndicate. Nobody got away with starting a crime ring in her hometown. "At least ask the sheriff if he thinks it's a good idea."

"You just want to go on a high-speed chase and run down the bad guys."

"Well, not really high-speed…" she hedged.

Tim's cell phone chimed. When he checked the message, his face fell. "Sheriff Gillespie wants me at the station now to make that report. I was hoping we could have lunch first."

"To discuss the case?"

"No, so I could take you on a date while you were still in town."

"On a real date?" Carol asked, needing to make sure she understood him correctly. That had been her every wish in high school, even though Tim was so much older, and he'd never looked at her that way then. They'd reconnected as friends, but the old dream was still there, lurking in the background. But it was better now because she knew Tim, not the teenaged fantasy she had of him.

"I pick you up, buy you lunch, we do some holiday window-shopping, and then I drive you home. That's as real as it gets," Tim said.

"And you're asking me now? When I have to go back to the city?" His timing was terrible.

"Rain check for the next time you're in town?" he asked. "I'd say 'or the next time I'm in Minneapolis,' but that probably won't be till the new year."

She'd wait for a date with Tim. "Definitely."

"I promise to text you updates every day. Even if there's no news on the case."

"Will you keep sending those bad jokes?"

"My jokes are never bad. And yes, I will. To help you develop your sense of humor."

"Heaven help us both, but I like this plan."

Her three-hour drive back to Minneapolis was long and cold. The next three days were just long and cold; the only bright spots in her hectic schedule were Tim's daily texts, all of which contained jokes because he had no news to report.

And then Thursday happened.

CHAPTER 7

TIM WAS VERY glad he hadn't blurted out his first impression of Carol's tag-the-tree plan. Who would ever think of putting a GPS tracker on an evergreen? But he'd kept her idea in mind, and Sheriff Gillespie hadn't immediately shot it down. In fact, the other man had been impressed.

"Carol French thought of that? Sam always said his baby sister was sneaky," Aaron Gillespie had said after taking Tim's attempted robbery report.

"She's not a baby anymore. She's trying to get onto the crime beat at her paper and thinks this might be her big shot. But she doesn't want to step on any law enforcement toes in the meantime."

"Creative and smart. She's a double threat."

"And pretty. Triple threat," Tim corrected. The only way he could see Carol as Sam's annoying little sister anymore was to look through his old yearbook. This new, grown-up Carol had his full attention for good reasons. Her being smarter than him only made Tim appreciate her more. "Is it worth looking into? Tagging the trees?" he asked.

The sheriff nodded. "It couldn't hurt. Let me know if you decide to do it. I'd like to have the information too. And I can liaise with other jurisdictions, if necessary," Aaron told him.

Tim was surprised to discover that Taylor Wear for Him carried the Never-Lost tags, although he shouldn't have been. The menswear store was the go-to clothing shop for anyone who was taking a winter vacation; it made sense for them to sell other travel accessories. Brian Taylor, the owner, laughed when Tim told him that the only things that might be taking a trip were his trees.

"Alright," Mr. Taylor said, his white teeth peeking out from his full beard. "I'm not one to judge. Set-up instructions are in the package. But do me a favor and let me know if any of your trees take a trip. It would be great advertising for the store."

Tim spent the first night charging the devices and testing the app he downloaded. Sam French offered to be his test chauffeur, driving the devices from Holiday Beach to Bixby since he had to drop off a special stained-glass window order. The tag's signal disappeared from his phone once Sam hit the town limits but popped back up again once he passed some open Wi-Fi spots in the next town. Tim expected as much. Cell service in the country was less reliable than in the city, and open Wi-Fi hotspots would be harder to find.

"It'll work," he reported when Sam returned to drop off the luggage tag.

"My sister's pretty smart," Sam said.

"She is."

"Make sure she isn't making a mistake, Tim."

"She isn't," he promised. Knowing he had Sam's approval didn't change his mind, but it felt good to know his friend had his back when it came to dating Carol. If he could only get the date to happen. Working every single day for the next two weeks snuffed out any chance he had of a social life, especially when Carol lived three hours away. It was going to be a challenge, but he was up for it.

He had a poor night's sleep on Monday and Tuesday since he only dozed, listening for his phone to sound the alarm. He was dragging on Wednesday, but his final shipment from Norman Tree Farm revitalized him to keep going throughout the cold evening. The new trees, with their extra-strong fresh-cut scent, enticed the families who were out shopping. Seven of them went to new homes that very night.

Tim spent hours tossing and turning and checking his phone to ensure the volume hadn't been accidentally turned off since the last time he'd checked it. Then, just as he felt himself finally drifting off, his cell phone blared to life. He blurrily stared at the screen, then punched buttons until he could see a blurry image of a rental truck backing into the open gates on his tree lot.

"Oh, no, you don't!" Tim tripped himself as he pulled on his jeans, his knees landing hard on his carpeted bedroom floor. He was pretty sure he put on his T-shirt inside out, but since he immediately covered it with a sweatshirt, he didn't bother to stop to check. He dialed the police station and let his phone ring as he pulled on his socks and boots.

The station's night operator promised to pass along his message to the officer on duty. By the time she repeated the tree lot's address, Tim was already outside and starting his truck.

"I took too long," he muttered to himself when he pulled into the lot. The thieves had locked the gate behind them, delaying him further in seeing how much they'd stolen. Security lights blazed to life with the new activity, illuminating the compound.

The half-empty compound.

Tim let his head drop to his chest. This was disastrous. A quick count showed forty trees were missing. There was no way Holiday Beach Christmas Trees would have a profitable season now.

Aaron Gillespie rolled up a few minutes later. He whistled as he took in the empty racks. "Wow, they weren't fooling around. Can you show me the video?"

The security system offered little new information. The rental truck's license plate was covered with dirt and snow. The two men loading the truck locked familiar, but he couldn't make out any details. The camera recorded the scene just fine, but dark knit caps and scarves, leather gloves, dark jackets, and jeans meant the thieves could be anybody.

The sheriff saw more than he did. "One older man, maybe a beard. One younger one."

"How can you tell?"

"By the way they move. The older man is in charge. He's giving the orders." Aaron watched until the truck was loaded and the pair drove away. "They knew exactly which trees they wanted. They also knew how to load them quickly and efficiently." He fell silent after that for a moment. "Do we know where they're headed?"

"How could I know that?" Tim demanded.

"I know it's four in the morning, but stay with me, Tim. The Never-Lost app. You did tag the trees, right?"

The app. Tim nodded vigorously, the movement

clearing his cloudy head. "Yes. I used the last two tags tonight. I put them in the biggest white spruces in the new batch." His cold fingers fumbled as he drew his cell from his pocket. Two minutes later, a blank map appeared on the phone's screen. "Nothing."

"So after all the trouble of buying it and installing it, it doesn't work?"

"No, it means they're between Wi-Fi sites. If they're headed south, we should get a ping when they drive through Bixby," Tim said without looking up. That was if everything worked perfectly. He couldn't imagine anybody stopping to dig through thick, prickly branches to search the trees for a two-inch metal attachment that might be hidden somewhere along the trunk.

Aaron gestured at the dark trailer. "Let's go inside and see which direction they're heading in. Then I can make some calls."

Four o'clock on a dark December morning had absolutely nothing to recommend about it. Tim coaxed the kettle to life, hoping a couple of mugs of instant coffee would keep them alive until the trees reported in.

They were half done with their beverages when his phone came alive. "Bixby," he confirmed. He zoomed in on the map. "And they aren't moving." He zoomed in closer. "That's the E.L.F. Evergreen Emporium." Tim hadn't expected the new kids on the Christmas tree block to be ripping off their competition.

"I'll call my counterpart in Bixby. If he catches them in the act, we can all go back to bed."

But the dots didn't stay put. Twenty minutes later, they were headed south again. "Sheriff, I don't think the Fergusons are the thieves. I think they just got hit." Tim stood, his decision made. "I'm going."

"They're out of my jurisdiction now," Aaron protested. "I can't help you."

"But I can get close," Tim protested. "I'll keep you informed every time they pop back onto the radar. We both know they're probably headed into Minneapolis. If you could give the metro police the heads-up, they can be there when the truck stops moving and swoop in." He didn't expect the SWAT team, but a handful of officers and a couple of police cruisers should be able to take care of the situation.

"I don't like it," Sheriff Gillespie said.

"You don't have to like it. I know I don't. You just have to make some calls." Tim's pickup had about a quarter of a tank of gas. That would get him halfway to the city before he needed to fill the tank, and the gas stations along the way should be open by then. "If I leave now, I'll only be half an hour behind them. I can make up some time. That's a big truck."

Aaron sighed. "Get going. Do *not* approach the truck. Call me whenever it's safe, when you stop, and if you change directions," he ordered.

Tim didn't know if the instant coffee had kicked in or if it was the adrenaline, but he was fully awake as he pulled onto the highway. Bixby flew by in a blink. The trees' tags appeared sporadically as the truck drove through larger towns, only staying on his screen long enough for him to note their location.

He'd fallen a little behind when he'd stopped for gas, but when the truck on his phone screen slowed down in St. Cloud, Tim was able to make up some time. "I think they're filling up," he reported to Aaron when he called in. "If they're stopping for breakfast, I could catch them."

"Or not," the other man said. "It's bad enough that

you're following them. No confrontations, Tim. Let me know when you get closer to Minneapolis, and I'll forward that information so the local LEOs can be on the lookout."

An idea popped to mind that Tim did not share with Aaron. "Will do, Sheriff."

After the truck hadn't moved for a full ten minutes, he felt confident enough to stop and put his own plan into action. The first time he dialed, his call went to voicemail. Tim didn't leave a message. He called back, hoping the non-stop ringing would be enough to rouse the person on the other end.

"French," a sleepy female voice answered.

"Up and at 'em, partner in crime prevention," Tim said.

"What? What!" Carol's voice was wide awake now.

"The lot got robbed again this morning. I'm following the luggage tag trackers, and they just entered St. Cloud. I expect them to be in Minneapolis within the hour. I thought you might want a heads-up."

"Hold on. I need pants."

Tim heard scrambling in the background. He figured Carol must have set the phone down while she got dressed. "I can't believe it's working. Does the sheriff know?"

"Yes. I'm giving him regular updates. I don't know where they're headed, but if you want to get to the north-east side of the city, you'll be in the general area when they arrive."

"You are the best boyfriend ever!"

Tim froze, fighting to keep his concentration on the road. "I am? Your boyfriend?"

"Well, we're like Batman and Catwoman working

together to solve a crime, but we haven't been out as Bruce and Selena on an official date yet."

"I have no idea what that means. But do keep telling people that I'm your boyfriend. I'll make it up to you after we speak to the police." Tim laughed as loud as she did. "That sounded better in my head."

"Too late. I'm going to tell everybody that our first date was after the arrests, and then I'm going to let you explain," Carol threatened.

"I need a promise first." Tim would never forgive himself if anything happened to her. Though he wouldn't have to worry about it for long since Sam would kill him. "I had to make the same promise to Sheriff Gillespie, so it's serious. Swear to me that you won't approach the truck."

"I won't. I want to report the crime news, not accidentally get caught up in the bust." Tim heard doors closing and muffled clicks. "Where am I going?"

Tim grinned. "Okay, girlfriend, do you know the gas station on Highway 10 at the edge of the city that has those killer sugar-covered donuts?" It was a favored pit stop for Holiday Beach locals as a clean place for a bathroom break and to load up on snacks for the drive home.

"Of course."

"Head that way, and grab yourself a donut. By the time you get there, I'll know if the thieves are sticking to their route to the city. If they are, I'll swing by, and we'll continue in your car in case they spotted my tail."

"Spotted your tail? I doubt they're even looking for somebody in the rearview mirror." Carol snorted with laughter. "See you soon, master spy."

CHAPTER 8

IT WAS FINALLY HAPPENING! It wasn't a traditional first date by any means since most of those didn't start with police involvement, but she was going on a date with Tim Olaffson. Carol stopped at the bottom of the stairs in her apartment building, then raced back to her unit to grab her DSLR camera. She could take pictures on her phone, but this was better. It seemed to take forever for her car to warm up and to scrape the frost from the windows, but five minutes later, she was on her way.

Morning rush-hour traffic was beginning to build, but most of it was coming into the city, and she was heading out. She made it to the gas station and filled her tank in case there was an extended car chase, and then began nibbling on her donut. Unfortunately, the station catered to commercial traffic, so she didn't know which truck she was looking for among all the vehicles coming in and heading out.

She'd backed into a parking spot in case she needed to make a quick getaway. It also gave her a perfect view of the parking lot. Carol timed it well; she'd only eaten half her donut when a familiar pickup pulled in beside her. Tim jumped out and quickly open her passenger door, and climbed inside. "What's the news, super spy?" she asked.

"They just started moving again." He stared at her donut. "I don't think we have time to get me a donut. I don't want to lose them."

"Lucky for you, I bought you one. You can eat and give me directions at the same time."

"I have to call Sheriff Gillespie first."

She listened to Tim's half of the conversation as she followed his directions into the city center. Tim didn't have a clue where they were heading, but she knew the area. Then she made a turn before he told her to.

"Where are you going?" he asked.

"To the Christmas tree lot in the Manufacturer Seconds' Discount parking lot. They're selling live trees for the first time this year," she told him. She'd like to add that she knew because she'd written an article on them, but the fact was the lot was close to her office, and she passed it every day.

"They stopped about six blocks up," Tim reported.

"That sounds right. Call the sheriff back and let him know we know their destination."

Carol pulled and parked on the side of the road a block away. Tim's fingers were clenched so tightly around his cell phone that she was afraid he was going to crack the case. She reached over and took his hand in hers. "Relax. The police know what's going on. Once they get here, we'll go over."

"It's Christmas trees. They aren't going to take it seriously."

"It's theft over five thousand dollars. They'll take it

seriously. And taking down a pair of Christmas tree bandits will be good press for them," Carol said. People's giving spirits ran high in December. The public would all come down on the side of the plucky independent Christmas tree lot owner once news of the bust came out. At least, they would all sympathize with Tim once she published her story.

Two police cruisers, lights flashing but sirens silent, pulled up beside the warehouse's fenced-in Christmas tree area. Carol carefully restarted the car and drove the remaining block so they could park in the parking lot next door. "Are you ready?"

Tim checked his phone. "Aaron says the police are expecting us."

The walk was short and quiet. Most of the warehouse's employees hadn't arrived yet, and the few that were there had gathered at the tree lot entrance.

"I'm sorry, sir, you'll have to come back later," an officer at the scene told them.

"My name is Tim Olaffson. Sheriff Aaron Gillespie of the Holiday Beach Police Department told me to identify myself to you because it's my property that was stolen."

The officer nodded. "Mr. Olaffson, do you really think you can identify your trees to the satisfaction of a judge? Otherwise, we're all wasting our time."

"I tagged them all. I also attached GPS trackers to two of them and can identify them on the company's app on my cell phone."

"That'll do nicely. Wait here, please."

Carol nudged Tim's arm when they were alone again. "I can't see who the police are talking to. Can you?" she asked. She couldn't imagine who would travel such a long distance to steal trees, but if they didn't want to be tied to the crime in the city, it made sense. It was also worth of the drive since selling two of the evergreens would pay for the gas for the whole trip.

The officer returned a minute later. "Come with me." He led them around the corner, where they came face to face with a blustering Nathaniel Norman and a silent Elton Wise.

"Tim, what are you doing here?" Mr. Norman asked.

"I was following my trees," Tim replied.

"Your trees? Officer, we do sell Mr. Olaffson his evergreens. We have receipts and everything. But these aren't his trees. They are direct from our farm."

"Then why are they tagged for the Holiday Beach Christmas Tree Lot?" Tim demanded.

"We were going to deliver them to you, but we needed them to fill this order. We will cut a new set for you, okay?" Mr. Norman said.

Carol had to admit that the older man was sticking to his story. Elton, on the other hand, had beads of sweat on his forehead, and it was twenty below outside. *Come on, Tim, let him have it*, she thought.

"No, Mr. Norman, it's not okay. Because you didn't tag those trees. I tagged them myself when you delivered them to me yesterday."

Now Mr. Norman looked nervous. "I'm sure there's some explanation."

"Do you also have an explanation for the two GPS transmitters we've been tracking from Holiday Beach to Bixby to here? Sheriff Gillespie has a copy of the app. He's been following their progress ever since my lot was robbed at four o'clock this morning by a truck that looks like yours. One that several people can confirm you've been using for deliveries all month."

Carol couldn't believe she had missed it. It was the same rental truck that she'd seen at the Norman Tree Farm when they'd visited a couple of weeks ago. It had the same summer lake scene painted on its side. Now she couldn't call Tim the super spy anymore, not when he was more observant than she was.

"Tim, can we talk? We can replace any trees that have gone missing and—"

"What about the ones you stole from the E.L.F. Evergreen Emporium?"

Elton raised his hands. "Forget it, Mr. Norman. We're done."

A new woman entered the scene. She was dressed in dark slacks and a red ski jacket with the store's logo on the chest. "What's going on here, Mr. Norman? I expected a delivery of white spruce trees, not a police presence."

"You would have been receiving stolen property," the police officer said. "Everything in this truck needs to be impounded and processed."

"Why would you steal from me, Mr. Norman? My family has had a good relationship with you for years," Tim asked.

The woman held up her hand to break into the conversation. "I'm Lorna Kent, the store manager. We don't have a history with Norman Tree Farm, but they had a good reputation, which is why we decided to buy from them when we set up our first Christmas tree lot. Will somebody please tell me what is going on?"

Mr. Norman sighed. "This is such a mess. I wanted to retire and sell the business, but my accountant told me it wasn't worth nearly as much as I'd hoped. I thought that if I could show a large profit this year, I could sell it for more money. We got the E.L.F. Evergreen Emporium contract and this one from Manufacturer Seconds' Discount, and they looked great on the books, but we didn't have the trees to fill the new orders. We raided next year's plantings, but we were still short. The only way we could come up with enough trees was to sell them twice. We delivered to our regular local customers, then recovered the trees and brought them to the city."

"And by recovered, you mean stole, right?" Carol said coldly.

"Their business insurance should have covered the losses. We were desperate this year. We only had to get through this month, and it all would have been over," Mr. Norman said.

"It's over now," Carol said.

The whole thing was much less exciting than television made it out to be. Mr. Norman and Elton Wise were handcuffed and put in the back of two police cars. The police officer in charge of the scene sealed the back of the truck, and another officer drove it away to the impound lot, she and Tim were told. Then she drove Tim to the police station to give their statements.

Her boss was not impressed when she called him to let him know she'd be late this morning. He was slightly mollified when she informed him she was at the police station getting information on a just-broken Christmas tree theft ring.

"I can drop you off at your truck, but then I have to get back. I'm sorry, I need to get this article written," Carol told Tim. It was the biggest opportunity she'd ever had at work, but at the cost of time with Tim. It wasn't a fun choice.

"I think we should ask Santa for better timing for Christmas, or we're never going to get that date," Tim said. "It's disappointing, but I understand. I have to get back to the lot and figure out how I'm going to end the season without the trees I need."

"I wasn't planning on coming out to Holiday Beach this weekend, but I am now. The lot closes at eight on Saturday. Make plans for eight thirty," Carol said. Their options in town would be limited, but if Tim was the man she thought he was, he'd come up with something.

"It's a date. A really good one," he promised.

CHAPTER 9

When Tim locked the gates on Saturday night, it was with a sigh of relief. He had six more days to go. As of eight o'clock next Friday, the day before the night before Christmas, the Holiday Beach Christmas Tree Lot would be closed for the season. The longest season in history.

He lost an entire day in Minneapolis dealing with the police. Tim had called in one of his temporary employees to open for him and had barely made it home in time to close. They'd been swamped with people wanting to hear about the robbery. They also bought more trees than usual to show their support, which was great but for the fact that it left him with next to no inventory.

Thankfully, Holiday Beach residents and his friends in Bixby came to the rescue. Emma and Lance called him to thank him for catching their thieves. They gave him the names of a couple of balsam fir tree farms who'd said that they'd be willing to sell some to Tim, given his unusual situation. The new kind of evergreens wasn't at all what his customers were used to, but everybody seemed determined to make the most of an awkward holiday situation.

But he'd made it through the week, and now it was time to take Carol out on their first official date.

Suits and fancy dresses would have to wait for another time. Tim wanted to give her something to remember when she was back in Minneapolis, something she couldn't find in the city. So he'd called in some favors, made a reservation, and had a plan that would knock her boots off.

Tim arrived at the French family home a couple of minutes before eight-thirty. Mary answered the door, and he whistled when he saw her. Carol's older sister was in a long-sleeved blue dress, and her hair was up in a fancy bun. "Wow, you look great, Mary. Where are you off to?"

"The River Street Community Center. I'm going to the Mistletoe dance inside," she said shyly.

"Have a great time."

"You have a good time on your date, too," Mary said with a giggle as her parents followed her out the door.

"Not too good a time," Mrs. French added on her way past. "You'll never know, we may decide to check on you."

"We'll look forward to it, ma'am." The grin Mrs. French wore let him know that they planned no such thing.

Carol met him at the door with her boots on, jacket zipped, and a bright fuchsia knit hat pulled firmly onto her head. "I don't have any skates, but I'm bringing extra socks," she said.

"Perfect. There's a rental place so you don't have to worry about skates."

The community center had flooded its outdoor skating rink in mid-November when the temperatures were consistently cold enough to maintain the ice. While it was mostly used for outdoor hockey practice and pickup games, Saturday evenings were reserved for adult skating.

Holiday music played over the exterior speakers, and bright spotlights lit the rink. An enterprising food truck set up in the community center's parking lot and catered to a steady stream of skaters who demanded hot chocolates and coffee. A sports store in Bixby came up with an SUV full of figure skates and hockey skates to rent to people who didn't have their own; they also held onto the renters' boots while they skated.

Tim found space on a bench for them to lace up their skates, then waited while Carol toddled back to the SUV to hand in her boots. When she returned, he held out his hand. "Ready?" he asked.

This was an even better idea than Tim originally planned. He hadn't counted on Carol being out of practice when it came to skating. Her ankles wobbled as she tried to find her balance, causing her to hold onto his arm for dear life. He loved it.

"I'm glad to see you survived the week. I was worried," she said.

"You called me every hour that first day."

"I wanted to make sure you were doing okay after finding out Mr. Norman was the bad guy."

"It wasn't a complaint." He'd appreciated every call, even if he'd had to let a few go to voicemail when he was driving. They'd talked long into the night more than once in the days following, trying to figure out how Holiday Beach Christmas Trees could recover and what they would have to do moving forward.

"How are the new trees working out?"

"Fine. Good, even," Tim said. "They aren't what we're used to, but they're good quality, and the customers seem to like them. Since Norman Tree Farm is up in the air for next year, I've already approached these new places about supplying us next year."

Carol nodded. "Norman Tree Farms is going to be a mess for a couple of years, especially since Elton and Mr. Norman tanked their reputation and raided next year's tree crop. If he can even find a buyer, he'll be getting a lot less than he would have if he hadn't tried to defraud everybody."

"For a moment, I considered buying it when it came on the market, but I figured that would be a little awkward," Tim admitted.

He caught her after she stopped short. "You what?" she asked.

"My grandparents don't want to run the tree lot again. They told me so this week. I've asked them to sell me the business. But one Christmas tree lot isn't enough business for a full-time income. I thought that owning both the source and the store might work." He'd been thinking about it a lot more than he was letting on. Working for the family was fine, but he wanted to make his own mark. If he owned Holiday Beach Christmas Trees, he could run it the way he wanted to without having to explain his choices. It would also give him the freedom and responsibility to collect all the profits. Then he'd have the potential to support a family if one came into the picture.

"That's big news, Tim. Congratulations."

"Unfortunately, as I said, I don't think that particular option would work. At least not until the criminal case is settled."

Carol squinted, studying his face carefully. "I sense a *but*."

Tim took a deep breath. "But another opportunity has

come up. Emma and Lance Ferguson have decided that the evergreen business is not for them. I can't blame them. They had a rough introduction. But that means there's potential to establish another lot in Bixby next year."

She understood immediately. He knew she would. "Tim, you could be a chain!"

He nodded. "It would be a big step."

"You could do it! Bixby would be a great second location. Close enough to check on but far enough away, so you don't overlap your customer base."

"It's just an idea at this point. I'm going to talk to the Fergusons in the new year."

She shook his arm. "Stop it. This is huge. Congratulations!" Then her shake turned into a death grip as her feet flew out from under her.

"Maybe this wasn't the best idea." They'd only made one circuit of the rink, and she'd almost fallen twice. "How about we move on to the second part of the evening?"

"I like that plan."

The patio of American Table could have sat unused from October to May, but the owners strove to wring every last day out of it. Which was why on Saturday nights, heat lamps and two large fire tables lit the space like a beacon on the cold winter night. Tim had reserved a table for two at the Polar Bar, and although they were early, they were still seated immediately.

"This is so cool. Is it new?" Carol asked.

"This is their second year. It's only open on Saturday nights. There's a limited menu. If you want to full thing, you have to be inside."

"What are our options?"

"Clam chowder, chicken noodle soup with a sourdough roll, or chili with cornbread." It was the perfect trio to ensure that diners didn't freeze to death and small enough portions so they wouldn't linger. Tim hadn't been there before himself. It wasn't exactly a place to go with the guys. But the lights twinkling off the snow and the piped-in Christmas music coming from the restaurant made it a magical date spot.

Their waiter must have had the same idea when he asked if they wanted him to take a photo of them. He handed back the phone, and Tim checked the picture. He and Carol had red cheeks from the cold air and huge smiles. He started a folder and added it as the first photo. He planned for it to be the first of many.

"Now that we've decided that I'm about to become a Christmas tree mogul, what about you? How did your editors like the story?" he asked.

"They liked it well enough to add my name to the crime beat roster. I'm the newbie, so I'll get all the low-importance and three-in-the-morning calls, but it's a start."

He knew her better than that. "You're dying for a three-in-the-morning call, aren't you?"

"I sleep with my phone under my pillow," Carol admitted with a laugh.

The disaster on ice and the quick bite to eat meant their date ended a lot earlier than Tim had anticipated. But it was long enough to linger on the Frenches' front step when he dropped her off.

"I have one week to go before I can think about taking you on a fancy date, but I think we had a good start today," Tim said. He couldn't wait to keep it going. Talking to Carol every night before he fell asleep was the highlight of his day. And when they did get to see each other in person, it was even better. He knew she had no plans to move back to Holiday Beach, but his expanding business opportunities could mean that he'd be spending more time in the city.

Anything was possible when it came to Carol, and Tim was excited for it.

"I'm looking forward to it. And to showing you around the city," she said.

"I don't know if I'm going to see you next weekend, so can I ask for my Christmas present early?" There was only one thing he wanted.

"Sure."

He leaned closer. "Merry early Christmas, Carol." She rose on her toes to meet his kiss, and it was sweeter than the hot chocolate they'd just had.

"Merry early Christmas, Tim."

It certainly was.

EPILOGUE

"Carol, honey, can you get the door since you're right there?"

"Sure, Mom."

News might happen after three o'clock on December twenty-fourth, but since the paper shut down over Christmas Day, she didn't have anywhere to report it. Instead, she'd left for Holiday Beach directly from her office, arriving at six o'clock, just in time for supper. She still had her boots on; Sam had grabbed her suitcase and taken it up to her old room, and Mary was finishing setting the table. Carol had no idea who would be calling at this hour.

"Tim?" she guessed when she opened the door. He was half hidden behind a massive bouquet of flowers wrapped in festive paper. "What are you doing here?"

"We invited him," her mom called from the kitchen. "His parents and grandparents are away for the holidays. Let him in!"

"Merry Christmas, Mrs. French."

"You can probably call her Ruth now," Carol said.

"Could. Won't," Tim said. "And hello."

She couldn't give him a kiss with all the scarves, jackets, and flowers between them, so she shed her coat and winter gear, handed the flowers off to Mary, then took his face in her hands. "Hello," she said, guiding him down for a kiss.

"Merry Christmas. I have your present in the truck."

"I have yours in my suitcase." They were new, so presents were still a bit awkward. She'd been struggling for the perfect gift until she found a massive mug saying "I'm the boss" at a gift kiosk in the mall. Next door to that was a fancy pen booth, where she found a pair of Christmas tree pens, and the one after that offered a variety of flavored hot cocoa mixes. It was the perfect gift pack for a man who had an evergreen empire to run during the cold months.

Sam only shot a few sideways glances at Tim when they sat down for supper. Since the Frenches saved the turkey for Christmas Day, the night before was a slow, social meal of fondue, with meat cooking in the beef broth and bubbling cheese ready for bread. Her family and Tim caught Carol up on all the holiday news of the last week as they ate.

"Mom got outbid on all of the teacups in the auction," Mary reported.

"But it was a good cause, so that means the food bank earned more money. Maybe next year will be my year," her mom said.

"I bought ten dollars' worth of tickets for the candy basket and didn't win," Tim complained.

"Me neither. And it was a lot of candy!" Mary agreed.

Since they had company, everybody agreed to open one gift in honor of their guests. Evidently everybody but

Carol had known that Tim was coming because they all had a little something for him, and he had presents for them. His parents got the flowers and the wine. Sam got a new pair of leather gloves to use in his stained-glass workshop. Mary got several skeins of wool for her hat-making.

Then Tim handed her a gift bag. The light item was a thin black leather wallet. When she flipped it open, she realized it wasn't for money. It had a clear case with a card that stated "Press" in bold black letters.

"You can hang it from a jacket pocket," he explained.

The heavy item was a large magnifying glass. "For finding clues? Or as a paperweight?" she asked. It was cute that he was marking her promotion.

"Both. Plus, it has a USB drive in the handle, so you can hide your backed-up files in plain sight. You can't be too careful when you're in danger of being scooped."

"Thank you. They're perfect!"

He didn't stay long after that. Instead, he thanked her family for including him and wished them all a merry Christmas the next day. "I'll call you tomorrow," Tim said quietly when Carol was standing with him at the front door.

"Are you going to be on your own?"

"No. Doug Mackenzie invited me to his place for turkey pizza and football. We'll have fun. But I'm taking you to breakfast on the twenty-sixth before you head back to the city, right?"

"You'd better. I brought my pancake-eating shirt."

"I don't know what that is, but I can't wait to find out."

Carol noticed that the living room had gone suspiciously quiet. She looked over her shoulder and caught a glimpse of her mother herding the rest of the family into the kitchen. Her mom was the best.

"You know, I had a huge crush on you when I was in high school. But this is better than I imagined," she said. They'd only walk a little way down this road together, but Carol knew that Tim was a man she wanted to go the distance with.

"For me too. It's only been a month, but it feels like much longer. Can you imagine where we'll be a year from now?" he asked.

She had a pretty good idea. And from the way he kissed her goodbye, Carol figured that Tim did too. "Merry Christmas to us."

THE END

PART FOUR

RING IN THE
NEW YEAR

Someone is getting engaged in Holiday Beach on a most memorable day.

RING IN THE NEW YEAR

CHRISTMAS MIGHT BE OVER, but the holiday season wasn't. Lucy Callaghan approached her car in the long-term parking lot of the Minneapolis airport and crossed her fingers in the dim afternoon light. She'd left it there for four days while she took a quick trip to see her family during the break between Christmas and New Year's Day. Today was the first of January, the beginning of a new year, and she wanted to start it on the right note. Now was the moment of truth. Could she make the drive back to Holiday Beach, or was she stuck in the city waiting for an auto club truck to give her dead battery a jumpstart?

Santa must have still been happy with her because the engine turned over without a problem. While she waited for it to warm up, she pulled her phone from her interior coat pocket and called up her favorite contact with frozen fingers for a quick video chat.

"I'm in the car. It started!" she yelled over the roar of the heater's fan.

"That's great news, but I have some that isn't as good."

Roy Wagner said. He looked a little tired on the small screen of her phone, but that wasn't surprising since he'd hosted a New Year's Eve party in his bar the night before. "There's a snowstorm rolling in, a Colorado low. It should be hitting Minneapolis about now, according to the weather stations."

Lucy looked through her windshield at the snowflakes fluttering to the ground. "That explains the dark skies. I think the edge of the storm has arrived, but barely."

"Do you want to drive home in this, or do you want to wait it out in the city?"

"Are you still planning our special New Year's Day celebration?" Lucy countered. Since he knew he'd be working on New Year's Eve, she had spent an extra day in Boston. They'd decided to ring in the new year together when she got home, and she didn't want to wait a minute longer than necessary.

"Um..."

"Everything was fine when I called you before I got on my flight," she said, wondering what had changed. The airport delay that had pushed her original arrival time back four hours shouldn't have caused him a serious problem.

"That was before I tried to turn on my stove. My oven is dead. So much for our Beef Wellingtons."

Lucy turned on the windshield wipers. She'd need them to keep it clear. "Why don't you take everything to my apartment and cook it there? Brooke should be home, and she has my spare key," she suggested.

"That would work! Okay, I'll pack everything up and take it over. Then I can refill your fridge with the fresh stuff I bought for you at the same time," Roy said. The look on his face was of immense relief, too much to be caused by just a broken stove.

"Is anything else wrong?"

"No." He shook his head for emphasis. "I was just really down at the thought of having to cancel our dinner. I also didn't want to have to call in an electrician and be charged double time on New Year's Day. I can wait till Monday now." He stood, and Lucy could see that he was in his living room. "I'll start packing our supper now. You drive safely, and if you need to pull over, do it. I don't want you to start the new year by needing to be towed out of a ditch. Be careful, sweetheart."

"I'll fill up on gas and snacks in the city and head straight home. I'll be fine," she promised.

They said their goodbyes, and Lucy psyched herself up for the journey. On a good day, going a couple of miles over the speed limit, she could make the trip in about two and a half hours. But with the weather reports coming in over the radio, she was looking at a three-hour drive if she could maintain the speed limit, and that would only be if she stayed ahead of the storm. The drive could be even longer if she let it catch up.

"Come on, self. Get moving. The sooner we hit the road, the sooner we can get home. After seeing how Holiday Beach did Christmas, I can't wait to see what Roy has in store for New Year's Day."

Her boyfriend had made her first December in her new hometown memorable. As a bar owner, Roy was used to working on holidays, serving customers who didn't want to spend notable evenings with family or friends or who didn't have anyone special to spend them with. But this was their first Christmas together as a couple, and Roy had made a special effort to give himself some time off. They'd attended choir concerts and done a Christmas-themed paint night. He'd even gone to a couple of holiday parties with her, although he'd had to leave those early to go to work. He made up for it when they'd thrown a private party at the Escape Room for their friends.

Lucy touched the sparkling studs in her ears. The beautiful gold shamrocks with the diamonds in the center had been her Christmas present from Roy. They matched the necklace he'd given her for her birthday back in the spring. They put the top-of-the-line snowmobiling boots that she'd bought for Roy to shame, although he'd sent her a picture of him wearing them while she'd been away.

They had exchanged other gifts too. Roy received a travel guide to America and the top one hundred sites everybody should see. He wasn't a big traveler, but Lucy was, and he agreed it wouldn't hurt to venture beyond the borders of Minnesota. So far, he'd crossed off the Mall of America and the Green Monster, the towering wall in Boston's Fenway Park. If everything went according to plan, they were going to drive to South Dakota to see Mount Rushmore in the spring before Roy's bar got busy with the summer crowds.

Lucy had received a beginner's pattern book for stained glass designs. She'd fallen in love with the various decorative windows around town and had mentioned possibly taking a class in the new year. Now she had several gorgeous patterns to choose from.

She'd filled her gas tank when she'd arrived in Minneapolis earlier in the week in anticipation of wanting to make a quick getaway when she returned. Her foresight paid off as she headed out of the city. She made one stop for a large coffee and snack food at a gas station at the edge of the city. Then she aimed her car for the highway. And home.

***

Waking up to a busted stove sounded like a bad thing, but it might have been a blessing in disguise. Roy Wagner carried three bags of groceries to his car and headed across town. He was glad Lucy suggested celebrating their New Year's Date at her apartment. It would work much better, even if she didn't know it.

The Escape Room had been busy from open to close during the week between Christmas and New Year's Eve. Although Holiday Beach didn't usually have a lot of tourists in the off-season, Christmas was one of the exceptions. The Dew Drop Inn next door had been fully booked, and between that and folks visiting family and friends in town, there had been parties every night filling every seat. Roy was ready for a day off and more than ready for his girlfriend to come back.

He still couldn't believe Lucy had only moved to Holiday Beach less than a year ago. When the property manager showed up at the hotel next door, she landed like a rock in a pond, sending ripples through the town. She was a changemaker, and they needed that. Since Lucy arrived, she'd spread her weird luck far and wide, and several people had benefitted. His assistant bar manager had won a trip to Los Angeles, a young man had a new apartment, and he was about to...

But not yet.

Roy pulled into a visitor's parking spot, noticing the lot had not been cleared since they'd had two short flurries earlier in the week. There wasn't much precipitation, but the snow fell over the top of his boots as he lugged his groceries to the apartment building. He buzzed Lucy's neighbor. "It's Roy. Can you let me in, please?"

A casually dressed blonde woman met him on the stairwell. "Is Lucy not answering her door? I thought she was coming home today," Brooke Portman asked. Roy knew she'd been Lucy's first friend in town, and the two had been close ever since.

"Her flight was late. She's landed but won't be here for a few more hours. She said that you'd lend me her spare key so I could cook supper here," Roy told her. It was nothing they hadn't done before.

"Sure, I'll grab it for you." Brooke led them up the stairs. "Do you think she'll make it home before the storm?"

"She was ahead of it when she was leaving the airport." They paused at Brooke's apartment. He looked around from the door while she dug in a drawer for Lucy's key. Roy saw that Brooke's Christmas tree was still up, with unwrapped presents piled underneath it. A stray bow and scraps of wrapping paper peeked out from under the sofa. An impressive number of junk food packages littered her kitchen table, but he had more on his.

"Aha!" Brooke triumphantly held up a shamrock keychain with a brass key attached. She slipped passed him and quickly unlocked Lucy's door, then stood aside as he carried in his bags. They both looked around quietly. The apartment was spotless, with not so much as a single bread bag clip on the kitchen counter. The coffee table in the living room was clear except for the television remote control. All Lucy's Christmas decorations were put away, including the four frosty gnome— not elf, she insisted—candle holders that had been on her kitchen table. Even the pillows on her sofa were artistically placed in the corners with artful karate chop dents in their centers.

"I hate your girlfriend," Brooke said.

Roy blinked. "Lucy said she was cleaning before she left." But this was more than he expected. He was afraid to touch anything. Unfortunately, her pristine place wouldn't stay that way once he started cooking.

"Maybe she's someone who insists on a clean house to start the new year fresh," Brooke offered. "I still hate her."

Roy set his groceries on the floor. The wine bottle in one bag clicked on the tile floor. A quick glance at the clock on the stove showed it was already after three o'clock. "I have to get cooking. Literally!"

Brooke chuckled. "Good luck with that. Don't make a mess of everything. I'll be home all afternoon if you need help. Or if you think of anything you want to tell me. Or—"

"Yes, yes, I get it. Goodbye, Brooke." Roy breathed a relieved sigh when the door closed behind her. He had a lot to do and only a couple of hours to do it. He unpacked everything he'd brought over from his house: rolls went on the counter, vegetables in the sink, meat into the fridge. Roy pulled his barbecue apron over his head and got to work.

***

Her knuckles ached from gripping the steering wheel so tightly. Lucy flexed her fingers one hand at a time before she returned to her sturdy grip. The storm had caught up with her much faster than she had anticipated. She didn't dare stop, not even for bathroom breaks, so her coffee had gone cold in the holder beside her. Snow in Boston was different than snow in the Midwest. This stuff was smaller and drier and hurt when the wind drove it into exposed skin. It was a cold burn rather than the wet cold of a heavy oceanside flake. It also made driving more of a challenge since her headlights turned the falling darkness into the image of a spaceship jumping into hyperdrive as snowflakes flew by like passing stars.

The highway sign on the shoulder said it was another ten miles to Bixby, with Holiday Beach a mere thirty miles beyond that. She was almost home.

An hour later, she passed her apartment building, no longer ahead of the Colorado low. The air was thick with snow, cutting visibility to a block. Her tires spun as she turned into the parking lot, then her entire vehicle slipped sideways, stopping inches before her passenger door was crushed by a snowbank. Lucy carefully slipped the car into reverse, hoping to back onto the road and try again, but she was out of luck.

Three bundled-up figures rushed over to her. She recognized Caleb Quentin, one of her tenants, and Trevor Gillespie, but not the third teenaged boy. She rolled down her window when Caleb gestured at her. "Need a push?" he asked.

"I do."

With the boys' help, she was able to creep into her reserved spot in the corner of the lot. The trio didn't hang around for thanks. They were off to Trevor's place to crash for the night, but they promised to push out any other stuck cars they came across during their walk.

Lucy thought she was home free until she stepped out of her car. One booted foot went one way, the other flew in the opposite direction, and her butt hit the pavement with a jarring thump. Thankfully, it was too cold for the snow to melt on contact, but the little bit that worked its way under her ski jacket and down the waistband of her jeans chilled her instantly. "So close," she muttered to herself.

It took her an unreasonable five minutes to trudge the short distance through the ankle-high snow towing her carry-on, then hauling it up the stairs. She was fumbling for her keys when she got to her door when it was suddenly opened from the inside.

She was a mess. She arrived at Logan International Airport two hours before her scheduled flight time, which had been delayed for another four. Then she spent over three hours on the plane and had a three-hour drive home after that. Her hair was flat, her make-up smudged, her clothes wrinkled and now wet. But Roy looked at her like she was the most beautiful thing he'd ever seen. "Welcome home, sweetheart."

Lucy threw her arms around him His warm hug made every second of her long travel day worthwhile. Unfortunately, Roy quickly let her go. "Why are you all wet?" he asked.

"I decided to make a snow angel in the middle of the parking lot before I came inside," she grumbled. Lucy shivered as she peeled off her coat and hung it on the rack by her door. She breathed deeply, happy to be home, and that was when she noticed the amazing scents coming from her small kitchen. "What am I smelling?"

"Supper. It's ready, but it can wait for a little while. You need to get warmed up first. Go shower and change. By the time you come out, you'll have a glass of wine waiting."

Her dark-haired, dimpled boyfriend was the best of

the best. Lucy kissed him again, pointed out the cabinet where the wine glasses were, and headed to her bedroom. She threw her wet clothes into her laundry hamper, laid out a new outfit on the bed, and darted into the bathroom wrapped in her long terry robe.

She was just turning on the shower taps when she heard a knock on her apartment door. Lucy stuck her head into the hall, but Roy waved her back inside. "It's probably just Brooke making sure you got home okay."

Brooke was a good friend, but a new one. Last year had been one of constant change. She'd started a new job in a new town and had found a new boyfriend. Lucy was ready for a year of stability now. She thought it would take a year to put down some serious roots. It had only taken nine months for her to realize she needed to make some longer-term plans, ones that included Roy. Her decision was easy. Roy's home was in Holiday Beach, and his business and family were too. He wouldn't want to leave. Since the town had quickly become home for her as well, she was happy to use that as a foundation for her future. And it all started today. "I'll be as quick as I can. I want to start celebrating the new year with you."

"Then hurry up!" he told her with a grin.

***

His lady looked exhausted. Roy hoped a hot shower would relax her so she could enjoy the evening he'd planned. It had taken him the whole week Lucy was gone to put the details together. The appetizers, the wine, the meal, the dessert, the post-dessert entertainment. Everything was her favorite. All his hard work was about to pay off.

As soon as he got rid of Brooke.

Roy didn't bother with the peephole, so it was his own fault when he almost took a set of knuckles to the nose as a tall girl reached to rap on the door again. The teenager, and she was barely that old, swallowed hard. "Is Miss Lucy home?"

A little voice coughed, causing Roy to look down and see the girl had an even smaller boy in tow. "Lucy's in the shower. Do you need help?" he asked. Roy didn't recognize either of them. Then again, he didn't know a lot of the kids in town.

"I'm Victoria Napier, from down the hall? I'm babysitting my brother. We had our Christmas tree lit, but all of a sudden, the lights flickered and then went really bright and then went dead," she said in a rush.

That didn't sound like a problem to him.

"We watched a video in class about Christmas trees and electrical fires and how they only take two minutes to burn up. Miss Lucy said she would always check our apartment for safety issues if we asked and my mom and dad aren't home..."

Roy nodded. It was probably nothing. But he'd seen those videos too. "Did you hear a *pphft* before the lights went dead?" he asked.

"No."

"Was there any smoke?"

"No."

Almost positively nothing. But the kid had done the right thing in getting an adult. "Give me a second." He indicated for the teenager to hold the apartment door while he went to knock on the bathroom door. "Luce, I'm going to check on something in the Napier's apartment. I'll be right back," he yelled.

"Okay!"

He really didn't have time for this. He had to change, reheat the Beef Wellingtons without overcooking them, and light the candles. But he couldn't ignore a kid asking for Lucy's help. "Tell you what. You two take me to your apartment and stay by the door, and I'll check the tree and the electrical outlet," Roy proposed. Victoria nodded so fast he could hear her Christmas bell earrings jangle. "Let's go."

As the two kids watched from the doorway, the first thing Roy did was unplug all the lights on the tree. The star at the top, which was still lit, went dark. So did the second string of lights. He examined the wall outlet on his hands and knees. There were no scorch marks on the plastic cover or the drywall, and the wall was cool to the touch. Roy looked at all the plugs stacked into each other. The second from the top was brown. He unfastened them all and, satisfied they were dead and not a problem, let them dangle from the tree. "I think it looks fine. Show your parents the plugs when they get home, okay? They should check each one individually."

"We will, thanks."

Roy jogged down the hall, checking the time on his phone. He had to turn the oven off in the next two minutes, or his entrée would be ruined. Then he had to change before Lucy got out of the shower and needed her room back. Not that Lucy would complain. She'd make some comment about how if it had been her tree, she would have blacked out the neighborhood. Sadly, it was true because her luck was usually that bad.

But not his. And, he hoped, especially not tonight.

Roy heard the shower shut off as he grabbed his shirt. He buttoned it at the speed of light, then slipped his pre-knotted tie over his collar and snugged it against his neck. His slacks, belt, and dress shoes went on next. When he heard her hairdryer hum to life, he bent slightly to check his hair in Lucy's dresser mirror, then returned to the kitchen, knowing she'd only be a few more minutes.

The dining table was as perfect as he could make it, with its tablecloth borrowed from the Atlas restaurant and his mother's China. He bought a bottle of Lucy's favorite red wine at Riesling and Brie. A red rose in a vase was the only decoration. He was ready. The Beef Wellington, double stuffed baked potatoes, and roasted asparagus were ready to be plated.

All he needed now was Lucy.

***

She wasn't blind. She'd spotted Roy's good clothing when she went into the bathroom and noticed its absence when she returned to her bedroom. Whatever he was planning, it was not a casual, relaxing dinner for two before a movie night. Lucy paused in front of her closet. Her red dress was a lighter weight than January required, but since they weren't leaving the apartment, it would be the perfect color to welcome the new year.

When she entered the kitchen, she was done up in fancy-date mode. She was pleased to see she wasn't over-dressed for the evening. "Hello, handsome." Her little apartment had never looked so intimate, with candles all over the side tables and along the television stand.

Now that she was warm and dry, she gave him the hug she hadn't when she first arrived. Roy squeezed her back tightly. "Welcome home."

He pulled out her chair, poured her wine, started the

music, and then stepped into the kitchen. "Can I help?" she asked.

"You can continue to sit there and look beautiful while enjoying your wine," Roy said.

"I do all the work in this relationship," Lucy joked as she reached for her glass.

He placed a basket of rolls to one side next to a pretty butter dish, then set her plate in front of her. Lucy breathed deeply. "It smells divine. I can't believe you cooked this."

"I still have some surprises up my sleeves."

He was just sitting down to join her when a pair of discordant car horns blared to life outside the window. His brow furrowed as he stared at her in confusion. "What was that?" he asked.

The horns quieted. "I asked if Mac has had any more trouble with his neighbors since the incident before Christmas." Lucy had thought that living in a small town was going to be boring, but the drama never ended. Mac Mackenzie was at war with the house being built next door to his.

"No. It seems construction shut down for the holidays, much to everybody's—" The dueling horns resumed their cacophony.

Roy shot his chair backward across the room as he stood up. "Please excuse me for a second."

Her bedroom and living room windows opened to the street. Roy paused for a minute to stare out the glass, then cranked the handle. "Hey, keep it down out there. Some of us are trying to have a nice supper!" he shouted.

"Get lost!" was the prompt reply before the horns started up again.

He turned to her. "One more second, sweetheart."

Then he took a deep breath to yell, "Sheriff Gillespie is in the building. Should I send him out to deal with your problem? Because I will." Lucy giggled at the implied threat. Roy might be able to do it; Aaron could be visiting Brooke.

She missed the reply, but Roy got the last word. "Take pictures and get yourselves home before this storm gets any worse. Deal with insurance in the morning. Happy new year." He lost points for having to crank the window shut instead of slamming it, but his intent was obvious.

He brushed the snow that had pushed through the screen onto the carpet and readjusted the curtains. Then he reclaimed his chair and reached across the table, capturing her hand with ice-cold fingers. "Now. Where were we?"

"Mac hasn't had any more trouble, and nothing else has happened in Holiday Beach since I left. I'm disappointed there's no other news." Surely somebody had done something noteworthy.

"There's one rumor making the rounds that will cause quite a stir, but nobody has been able to confirm it yet. I think the situation is going to be decided one way or another by tomorrow, though."

Lucy loved good gossip. "Do tell!"

He squeezed her hand a little tighter. "Lucy—"

Knock knock.

"Are you *kidding* me?" Roy stood again. "Don't go anywhere."

With visibly forced patience and a growl he didn't hide, Roy left Lucy for the third time that evening. This time, there were no harsh words, and nobody asked for her. In fact, she didn't hear anything but a sigh, and Lucy wasn't sure who it came from.

Roy shut the door firmly. She couldn't be sure, but he might have been talking to himself. He sat down and reached for her hand again. Then he waited.

And waited some more.

When nothing interrupted him, he looked deeply into her eyes. "Lucy, I have to ask you something."

***

Please don't let there be any more interruptions, Roy silently pleaded. He had to get through this. Potential Christmas tree fires, car accidents, and nosey neighbors were enough to drive a man over the edge.

"Okay," Lucy said.

Okay, what? Oh, right. The thing. "The last year has been the best year of my life," Roy began. He'd practiced to get the words perfect. "Holiday Beach, my whole world, got bigger and brighter after you moved to town. You're smart and funny and beautiful, and each day I get to spend with you is a gift. You already know I love you, but I want more. I want to be sure I can spend every day with you for the rest of my life." He drew a velvet box from his pocket and opened the lid. "Lucy Callaghan, will you say yes and make me the luckiest man in the world?"

He knew Lucy's taste defaulted to practical, but she'd loved the shamrock necklace he'd given her for her birthday. Roy already had the matching earrings waiting as a Christmas present, so when he decided to ask her, he returned to the same jeweler to find a ring in a similar style. It looked delicate but was actually strong and solid, just like Lucy.

"Roy, it's beautiful."

"You can't have it unless you say yes."

"Of course, yes. Yes, I'll marry you," she exclaimed. "I'd marry you without the ring, Roy. I love you."

The ring slipped easily onto her finger. And Lucy slipped easily onto his lap, where he kissed her. "I was worried that this evening would never happen," he confessed. "So much went wrong. Your flight getting delayed, the oven breaking."

"Me almost getting stranded because of the storm," she continued. "Victoria Napier's tree incident."

"Me almost getting arrested because those two idiots outside kept interrupting me."

"Well, I'm not letting you take the ring back even though I did say yes. It's beautiful, Roy." Lucy said. She held out her hand to admire it, and the diamond caught the flickering flames from the candles in the room.

"You make it look beautiful." He kissed her again and was heartened by the fact he was now kissing his fiancée, his soon-to-be wife. Most of his friends had married a decade younger, but he hadn't found anybody he wanted to spend his life with until Lucy.

"I'm glad you were able to ask me without another interruption," she said. "Speaking of which, who was at the door that last time?"

"Travelling encyclopedia salesman."

"Royal Wagner!"

"Nobody we have to worry about right now. Don't you think we have more important things to talk about than nosey neighbors?" Brooke, and likely Aaron, would come to offer congratulations soon enough, and they'd spilled the news to some other friends who would brave the weather to celebrate with them.

"Nosy neigh..., was that Brooke at the door?"

"Brooke, who? We're the only two people in the world tonight."

"Roy! Did she know you were going to propose tonight? She never said a word."

"She helped me figure out your ring size. And I swore her to secrecy." Not that Brooke would have deliberately spoiled his surprise. But she'd been so excited to be part of his plan that she might have let something slip. When she'd come knocking on Lucy's door that evening, she'd been bursting with happiness. It had taken a stern warning to convince her that he hadn't done the deed yet because of all the delays. But Brooke had threatened to come back later.

"No wonder I only got one-word responses to my messages when I was away this week," Lucy confessed with a laugh. "I thought she was overwhelmed at work because of all the holiday guests at the Dew Drop Inn."

"We can let everybody know tomorrow," Roy said. "I'd rather have you all to myself tonight. We can—"

A knock on the door interrupted his thought. And their evening. Lucy smiled and kissed him before she ran to the door. She flung it open, and as he expected, Brooke and Aaron stood in the corridor. Aaron held a bottle of champagne at his side. The men exchanged smiles while Brooke squealed in delight as Lucy showed off her ring. "You might as well come in," Roy said. "I don't suppose we're going to get rid of you tonight."

Aaron grinned sympathetically. "I sat on Brooke for as long as I could, but she demanded we come and celebrate your engagement. I hope she waited long enough this time."

"Barely."

"Then we're right on time. Congratulations. Lucy's a prize."

Roy happily accepted the offered hand and the good wishes. "She sure is."

Brooke put her hand on his shoulder, then stood on her toes to kiss his cheek. "Congratulations, Roy. I'll be right back."

She darted away, and Lucy slipped in to take her place. "Apparently, she made us an engagement cake. Also, Mickey is hiding out in her apartment waiting for the green light, along with a few more friends."

"I hope you're ready for a party," Aaron said. "I'll go help Brooke. We'll be right back."

"I had hoped tonight would be just the two of us," Roy admitted when they were alone again. He wanted to get married within the year. He didn't need a big wedding; he only had his brother and one of his grandparents. Lucy, on the other hand, had tons of family. They needed time to plan. "But it's nice that we have so many friends who want to celebrate our good news."

"I get to spend the rest of my life with the man I love. I can spare them one evening," Lucy said, her sandy-brown hair resting on his shoulder. "Today hasn't been what I expected, but I think we're going to have a very happy new year, Roy."

"I love you too. It's going to be the happiest year ever."

THE END

ABOUT THE AUTHOR

Elle Rush is a contemporary romance author from Winnipeg, Manitoba, Canada. When she's not travelling, she's hard at work writing books which are set all over the world. From Hollywood to the house next door, her heroes will make you sigh and her heroines will make you laugh out loud.

Elle has a degree in Spanish and French, barely passed German, and has flunked poetry in every language she ever studied, including English. She also has mild addictions to tea, her garden, bad sci-fi movies, and HGTV.

Keep up-to-date with new releases and more by signing up for her newsletter at **www.ellerush.com/newsletter**.

SWEET CONTEMPORARY ROMANCE

Holiday Beach (also in paperback)

Shamrocks and Surprises

Pumpkins and Promises

Tinsel and Teacups

Fireworks and Frenemies

North Pole Unlimited

Decker and Joy

Hollis and Ivy

Nick and Eve

Rudy and Kris

Ben and Jilly

Frank and Ginger

North Pole Unlimited Collections (also in paperback)

Collection 1 - Decker and Joy, Hollis and Ivy

Collection 2 - Nick and Eve, Rudy and Kris

Collection 3 - Ben and Jilly, Frank and Ginger

Hopewell Millionaires

Doctor Millionaire

Fall a Million Times

A Million Love Notes

Royal Oak Ranch

The Cowboy and the Movie Star

The Cowboy and the Pastry Princess

The Cowboy and the Constable

<u>Resort Romances</u>

Cuban Moon

Mexican Sunsets

Dominican Stars

Mayan Midnights

Complete series 4-book box set

COOKBOOKS

Heartmade Collection

Brunch

Mains and Sides

Holiday Table